PENGUIN BOOKS

The Blind Blonde With Candles In Her Hair

Born in Auckland in 1932, C. K. Stead made his name as one of the new New Zealand poets of the 1950s and 60s, and developed an international reputation as a critic. He was also known during those years as a short-story writer and editor. His novel *Smith's Dream* appeared in 1971 and was filmed as *Sleeping Dogs* in 1977. In the same year appeared Stead's Katherine Mansfield's *Letters and Journals,* which continues in print.

In 1986 the author took early retirement from the University of Auckland Professorship of English he had held for twenty years. He holds a doctorate from the Universities of Bristol (PhD) and Auckland (LittD) and was awarded the CBE in 1985 for services to New Zealand literature. He is the only person to have won the New Zealand Book Award for both poetry and fiction, and one of only two New Zealanders elected a Fellow of the Royal Society of Literature.

Among Stead's novels are *All Visitors Ashore, The Death of the Body, The Singing Whakapapa* and *Villa Vittoria. The Singing Whakapapa,* published by Penguin in 1994, won the fiction section of the New Zealand Book Awards in 1995.

Stead is married with three children and several grandchildren.

The Blind Blonde With Candles In Her Hair

Stories by

C.K. STEAD

PENGUIN BOOKS

Acknowledgements

Landfall, Metro, Sport, Vital Writing 1 & *3*;
also *Chelsea Hotel* (Germany), the *London Magazine*,
the British Council's *New Writing 5* and *6*, and the
Faber Book of Contemporary South Pacific Stories.

'Of Angels and Oystercatchers' first appeared in
The Inward Sun, dedicated to Janet Frame.

PENGUIN BOOKS

Penguin Books (NZ) Ltd, cnr Airborne and Rosedale Roads, Albany,
Auckland 1310, New Zealand
Penguin Books Ltd, 27 Wrights Lane, London W8 5TZ, England
Penguin USA, 375 Hudson Street, New York, NY 10014, United States
Penguin Books Australia Ltd, 487 Maroondah Highway, Ringwood,
Australia 3134
Penguin Books Canada Ltd, 10 Alcorn Avenue, Toronto, Ontario,
Canada M4V 3B2

Penguin Books Ltd, Registered Offices: Harmondsworth,
Middlesex, England

First published by Penguin Books (NZ) Ltd, 1998
1 3 5 7 9 10 8 6 4 2

Editorial services by Michael Gifkins & Associates
Designed & typeset by Egan-Reid Ltd, Auckland
Printed in Australia

Contents

Concerning Alban Ashtree

❦

O N THE BUS THIS EVENING I THOUGHT, 'ANYTHING
can look like a movie of itself – i.e., unreal.' Can I
recover the buoyancy of that thought? I was leaving
the Quinton campus for my apartment across the river. There
was snow on the fir trees and on the steps of the Faculty Club,
the lawns and gardens were buried under it, it bulged on the
houseroofs, it was banked thick over everything except the
brown ragged-edged strip of roadway kept clear by snow-
ploughs, and the tracks dug from sidewalks to doors by
householders, and the icy sidewalks themselves over which I
and the students skittered to the bus-stop.

I will call them 'my apartment', 'my office' – I have them
on loan, one, the office, looking over snow-bound fir trees
down to the frozen river, the other, the apartment, looking
from the city down to the river and up to the university. If I
could occupy both at once I could wave out to myself, and
would do it to relieve the loneliness. I am a Distinguished
Visitor for just a few months, introduced to everyone, forget-
ting all their names, avoiding them all because avoidance is my
habit, and hungry for company.

A Distinguished Visitor is worth quite a lot of money – or a
lot by his own modest standards. This morning an account
opened in my name to receive $4800. 'Age?' the young lady

asked, establishing details for future identification. 'Forty-eight,' I honestly replied (one year for each hundred dollars). 'Height?' 'Six feet.' 'Weight?' 'Seventy kilos.' 'Colour of eyes?' 'Blue.' 'Colour of hair?' – and before I had replied she looked up and wrote 'grey'. 'Grey at the edges,' I wanted to protest. But on the other hand there's not a lot more than edges left; and in any case I was wearing my leather peaked cap in the style of Helmet Schmidt.

What was the movie I seemed to see myself cast in as I came out of the Hubert Harrison-Jones Memorial Building on to the Harriet Harrison-Jones Memorial Drive to catch my bus into Quinton? It was of course a North American campus movie. A student – a girl student – with pink fingers searching for her bus pass ought to have accidentally spilled the contents of her bag on my lap. Apologies. She's flustered. The bus starts. She falls back half into the seat beside me, half on my lap among the books. More apologies while her things are gathered up and returned to her bag. We talk about the weather. She discovers I am a visitor. Not the Distinguished Visitor, Helmet Schmidt? I admit it's so. She's so pleased she tells me at once about her boyfriend. He was supposed to meet her this evening. Didn't show up. Unreliable. She agrees to have dinner with me. Later in the week (to condense this tedious and trivial narrative) we go skiing together and finish up in a chalet naked in a barrel of hot water soaping each other's nipples . . .

No student fell into my lap this evening, none spoke to me or recognized me as the Distinguished Visitor Helmet Schmidt. I don't complain of this nor believe it ought to have been otherwise. I note only that it is these little divergences that make the reality of the movie, or (as this evening) the reality of reality (you take your choice according to mood, circumstance, and that buoyancy I spoke of) unreal.

Now it's night and out there the northern prairies weather

means business. It's minus 27 Celsius, the scraped sidewalks hard with ice, and you fight your way along inside a big old German tweed coat which adds kilos to that figure of seventy so lightly offered this morning, and looking like a big old German. But it's no longer the Helmet Schmidt cute cap in wapiti leather peaked over your northern blue eyes and grey-edged hair but a red blue and white skiing toque tight down over brow and ears, your scarf over your chin, and the breath between faintly holding the cold at bay from that chiselled (or chisel) nose. Yet in empty Archibald Square you hear 'Les Bicyclettes de Belsizes' piped to the icy skies and a scrape-scraping to its rhythm. Surely not? – but yes, two hardy teen-agers in the half-light and togged to the eyebrows are skating on its flooded-and-frozen centre. The weighty German tweed is doing its winter work but the frightful chill is getting into the toque and through the shoes, your trousers at and below the knee feel as if they've gone over to the enemy, and you push desperately into the little Chinese restaurant at the door of which you hesitated last evening and turned away because then as now there were no customers – not one. But the dish when it comes is huge and cheap and, with no frills, distinctly and edibly Chinese.

Warm and replete you're ready for the short battle homeward. There is, you reflect, something to be said for a climate that makes simply setting forth an adventure – never mind setting forth for what. Your apartment is on the 12th floor and you will soon be drifting to sleep with the curtains open, looking at the lights of the city and the snow falling on to your balcony. Contrarily, these past days, through all the invasions of melancholy, loneliness, disorientation, has come the old absurd ebullience, the unreasonable sense that life is its own reward.

This war between vanity and convenience, the cap and the toque, has led me to inspect my ears in the mirror. I conceived of them, if at all, as small and neat. In fact they appear rather large and sprout a few untoward and random hairs; but they lie flat against my head. At 8.30 this morning on Channel 4 which gives constant print-outs of the weather I watched the temperature dropping and rising between minus 29 and minus 30. Two hours later it was up to minus 22 Celsius. In between I had walked, capped, two blocks to the Hudson Bay Company for supplies. The ears burned and froze and stung and ached. Two flaps of flesh one has scarcely acknowledged as existing in their own right are bidding to become determinants of behaviour.

This morning too I did my balcony experiment – a dish of water there, and one in the deep freeze. As expected, Nature won. There was a skin of ice on the balcony dish in the time it took to walk across the room and back. Minutes later the Kelvinator dish hadn't begun to freeze. So, you darlings in the South Pacific, to whom I wrote that stepping out here is like stepping into a coolstore – revise it, please. And remember the air in this deeper freeze moves. It's what they call a wind-chill factor and it's why God designed you flap-eared – so you would have fair warning. When some oil-rich sheikdom invites me to its university as a Distinguished Visitor and provides me with a handsome apartment I will of course fry an egg on the balcony rail and another in a pan on the stove, and again, no doubt, Nature will triumph.

But it's Sunday afternoon I've a need to record. I was taken to the home of the chairman of Quinton's Department of Comp Lit (my host department) to meet the chairman and his family and some of the members of his staff. Chairman Hyde is big, sandy-haired and slow-spoken. His wife is small, quick, pretty, still youthful, shy at first, but soon the confidence appears, and with it the pride, and the impatience. She's almost certainly cleverer than her chairman, and has recently completed her PhD. She tells how someone phoned recently and asked, 'Could I speak to Dr Hyde,' to which she replied, 'Which of them do you want?'

Across the street the neighbours are shovelling snow off the roof. Paths have been dug to the sidewalk. More members of the department arrive. There is one, Eugene Fish, who has a thin moustache and the look of a band leader of the 1920s. His wife is plump and must once have been pretty. She's still pretty, but plump. Her dress has a design of tiny shoes that run around it in circles. She's one of those faculty wives who cause embarrassment by offering perfectly ordinary and sensible domestic observations and reminiscences. She's shy and never raises her voice much or moves her lips, but it's obvious she's a compulsive talker once set in motion through a gap in the conversation, and Eugene Fish covers for her with quick loud quips, like a back-up gun in a Western movie.

There is also a big man, an American, Hank Judder, who arrives on skis wearing mukluks and a large Indian fur-lined coat with a hood. He's a poet and lives in the woods out of town with his wife who weaves and does Indian craft work. Judder hasn't sat down before he's wanting me to agree that the eighteenth century is the sanest century. I feel he's checking me out before deciding to stay. I say, 'The sanest is the most insane,' at which he looks doubtful, and probably disappointed; but he accepts a drink from chairman Hyde and sits down chewing on my reply.

Faculty talk goes on, making considerable use of numerals. It's like that story about the monks who've lived so long together they've reduced all their jokes to numbers. 'Fourteen,' one monk says, after a long silence, and they all laugh. 'Twenty-two,' says another, capping the first, and they fall about slapping their sides. In faculty talk the numbers are courses – 3.307 the Literature of Silence; 2.903 Comparative Semiotics; 4.747 Frontier Feminism; 3.208 the Literature of Sexual Harassment. So it goes. 'We need to take another look at 1.425.' 'I've got to get through 2.901 before I can begin to think about that.' 'But that won't be until the next session.' 'The chairman's setting up a committee anyway, to look into all the 3s.' 'Did that student in 4.301 get hold of you?' 'Someone told me your 2.222 lectures have been brilliant this semester.'

Out there a squirrel is rippling along a bough, and I remember I've read somewhere that the word 'squirrel' comes from the Greek and means 'shadow tail'. The youngest Hyde describes to me the animal's regular path – over the woodshed at the back, along the fence, across the roof, down the elm bough . . . He asks me about animals in New Zealand. I tell him about the possum I feed. He tells me about the skunk that got under their porch. In a minute the numbers are dropped, everyone is exchanging animal stories. A moose has been seen this year down on the frozen river. The lady with the little coloured shoes walking in circles around her dress tells how she got up in the night and saw 'a nice dog' in the moonlight on the snow. 'And then it put its head back and . . .' They all laugh. Junior Hyde explains to me that the 'nice dog' was a coyote. Hank Judder explains his problems with bats which maybe ought to be killed because they're said to carry rabies but which at close quarters have appealing faces. There's a story about bears one summer on the shores of one of the lakes . . .

Numberless, we seem more relaxed. The animals have humanised us. The drinks may have something to do with it as well. Outside there is the scraping of shovels on paths and sidewalks. I resolve inwardly, solemnly, never to write about these people. Cross my heart and hope to die. Chairman Hyde asks me whether I'm finding Ashtree's office comfortable.

Already Ashtree has taken my fancy. There's that shelf of handbooks on writing in his office – *The Practical Stylist, On Writing Well, Styles and Structures, The Writer's Control of Tone, A Handbook of English, The Canadian Writer's Hand-book, The Complete Stylist.* Why should a distinguished Canadian poet keep all that stuff on his shelves? I suppose all it means is that he teaches one of those courses designed to turn sow's ears into silk purses (I imagine a text called *The Sow's Ear's Handbook*) – but on the other hand, could it be that all this armoury is designed to make a better writer of Ashtree? Or to get something special into shape? For the purposes of tenure perhaps?

I tell chairman Hyde the office is comfortable, the view fine. It's a room, of course, hermetically sealed. The windows can't be opened and you must take the weather sent to you through pipes. I'm told that on the other side of the building the combination of piped weather and natural sunshine turns the offices into something like a sauna parlour. With snow-drifts heaped up against the unopenable double panes, and great icicles hanging from the eaves, they sit sweating and trying to cool themselves with electric fans. I have no such problem. But does Ashtree mind my occupancy while he's away on leave? Was there a problem of some kind?

My question produces what I think might be a moment of awkwardness. Is chairman Hyde embarrassed? Quick as a pretty ferret his lady, Dr Hyde II, says if the Distinguished Visitor is comfortable then there's no problem. And she offers to refill his glass. I'm reeling as it is, not used to drinking in the afternoon. Maybe that's why I persist. I mention the letter I've had from Ashtree. 'Dear Professor Bulov,' it began. 'I have just been informed that you, as Distinguished Visitor to Quinton campus, have been assigned to my office for your personal use throughout the duration of your stay.' I think some of those handbooks might have been profitably brought to bear on that sentence, but Ashtree was writing under pressure. He went on to explain that there had been 'no consultation'. He had no prior warning that someone would be 'poking about' in his office, which (he continued) like

13

everyone's, he supposed, contained papers which were 'personal and private'. In particular he would be grateful if, 'instantly upon arrival', I would turn the key in the top of the filing cabinet and hand it (I assumed he meant the key, not the cabinet) to Mrs Merrill at the departmental office for safe-keeping. The top key, I would find, locked all four drawers at once.

I responded to this as to an electric prodder. Already when his letter reached me I had been in occupation three days. It was too late for action 'instantly upon arrival'. But in those three days I hadn't so much as looked at his filing cabinet. I don't believe I noticed it was there. Now I sprang into action – out of the chair in which I was reading his letter, across the room, turning the key at once that was sticking out of the top of the cabinet, guiltily locking its contents away from my own prying gaze and taking the key directly to the imperturbable Mrs Merrill who said it would go straight into the depart-mental safe.

I convey something – a little – of all this to the Sunday afternoon, but there's no response. If there's anything odd about Ashtree they're covering well for him. 'I should have warned the poor guy,' chairman Hyde admits. 'I thought I did warn him. There's so damned much to remember these days.'

After the others have gone I'm retained, along with Hank Judder for dinner with the family. There's a dispute about whether it's true the bathwater goes down differently in the Northern and Southern Hemispheres – clockwise in one, anti-in the other. I try to use my wine glass as a globe to show that a clockwise spin is anti-clockwise when looked at from below. I spill my wine. The children insist the difference between hemispheres is real, and they have a name for the phenom-enon. Hank Judder asks me about my tastes in music. His are classical, mine romantic, and my voice vanishes inside itself as I lumber into an honest admission of what Wagner does to me.

The days are going by. I clamber into toque (the Helmet Schmidt look has admitted defeat) scarf coat gloves and go out to buy the few things I need. I sit staring at the long green hair of the carpet in my apartment and at the snow falling in the streets, thinking of nothing. Quinton seems unreal, so does New Zealand. I'm tired, sleep too long and wake tired. I force myself out of doors into the bracing air, crunching over the ice, to wake myself. Sun shines on the snow, the huge icicles hanging at the corners of the Faculty Club glisten, the skiers glide by among the trees, the brief day is dazzling and beautiful but the cold drives me indoors again. I write letters home but there's little to report. In the afternoons I sit in Ashtree's office watching the shadow cast by this slope climb the other beyond the river towards the base of my apartment tower. Down-river there are factory chimneys casting white smoke into the icy blue which seems edged with green at sundown. In the far distance there's a single gas flare. It's hard to imagine the river, a quarter of a mile or more wide, is still flowing down there under its ice.

Somewhere under the faces people in the department present to me I sense warring factions. I try not to identify them, not to guess where I belong in them or for whom my invitation may have been a triumph and for whom a defeat. The long-tailed magpies dart about in the empty trees and I wonder what they find to eat. Melancholy loves me dearly and wants to hug me to her heart.

Ms Valtraute, on the other hand, is probably not interested. She presents a paper on the poetry of Alban Ashtree to the Graduate Seminar on Canadian Literature. Being a feminist, she takes a strong line with certain aspects of Ashtree's work. His 'Muse obsession', for example. His 'Snow-White Goddess', she calls it. She admires him for his independence – especially his independence as a Canadian (lucrative offers from US campuses have been rejected). She loves his sense of 'the divine in the derelict'. She approves of the way he has shifted the central image of Canada away from open spaces to the urban scene, yet without losing all sense that 'the cold wastes are still there, challenging the imagination'. But in human relationships he is 'cock-eyed' – and she means it (she adds fiercely) quite literally.

I've always been drawn to strong, intelligent, verbal, not to say literary women, as some men are drawn to rock-climbing, or hang-gliding, or canoeing down rapids. And Ms Valtraute is tall with a beautiful freckled nose, a perfect mouth, keen clear observing eyes and thick red-gold hair. She plans to write her thesis on sexual politics in selected poets of the Commonwealth and I'm wondering where in her life sexual politics, as she calls it, ceases to be politics and is permitted to re-inhabit its long social and biological history.

This afternoon is Friday and today the sun has failed to shine. Cloud presses down on the tall buildings across the river, snow is falling, and cars crossing the bridge have their lights on. An awful silence has descended over the department, signalling the onset of a weekend in which I have nothing to do, no one to talk to. My eye goes around and around the room. A student from Bangladesh knocks and asks to borrow a stapler. I find one in Ashtree's desk. The student uses it, thanks me and vanishes into the silence. My eye, going around again, falls on drawer three (counting from the top) of Ashtree's cabinet. It seems to be protruding a few millimetres. I pull at it idly and it opens. I slam it but it won't shut. The bolts, closing downward from the top, have left drawer three unlocked. I rush out for Mrs Merrill. She's gone, as is everyone else. It seems I'm to spend a weekend with that naked lady, the filing cabinet of Alban Ashtree, baring her bosom or her belly at me.

My thoughts return – I return them there myself, under strict instruction – to Ms Valtraute. Her first name is Libby. A few nights ago she sat three rows in front of me at Quinton's National Film theatre. She was wearing a coat with a fur-lined collar and in the half light it reminded me of something out of my past – or was it out of the forbidden filing cabinet? (already I'm uncertain). I was in Denmark in late autumn, a little snow was falling and I was standing outside a discotheque called Locomotion with a lady whose name was Bodil. We had been dancing in the discotheque – God knows why. Bodil was a respectable bourgeois Danish lady with a husband in banking and two delightful children. But I had been a visitor (Distinguished? – yes, I think so) and she had been entertaining me. First dinner (teaching me how that Danish table with its apparently random offerings is to be approached in the proper order) and Danish beer, then wine because I had wanted it, and finally, by no very clear progression, Locomotion, where Bodil feared she might be seen by some shop assistant or bank clerk who would recognise her, but where she danced like a demon. And now we were standing in the flurries of light snow, outside the discotheque and down the road from my hotel, and Bodil was drawing the pale fur collar around her throat and declining to kiss me. 'I am very hot-blooded,' she explained, as if it were a deficiency. 'If I kiss you I get excited.' She was about to get into her car. I took hold of her – it was just a big friendly hug in the snow flurries, my mouth somewhere between the collar and the throat, touching both. I felt her resist and then relax. She sighed, 'Goodnight Mr Dancer,' she said. And she got into her big German Ford, waved a small gloved hand, and drove away.

I enjoy shopping, and buy more than I need. It's the standard form of stimulation, isn't it, for people who live inside a system of protective cocoons. But I've neglected to buy soap powder. I decide to manufacture some out of the airline toilet soaps I've collected along the way. I choose UTA and it takes almost half an hour sitting at a table with the bread knife turning the little bar of soap into fine Lux-style flakes. I've done that and the machine's already into its second rinse before I remember that this apartment block has a shop which is open on Sundays.

Some kind of tussle goes on in me about whether I should go to my office this afternoon – to Ashtree's office. There's nothing else to do, it's true. And yesterday for the first time I proved to myself it's possible to go there on foot. I bought one of those knitted hats which conceal a face mask you can pull down to your chin, with gaps for eyes and mouth. Crossing the long bridge over the river I had to pull down the mask against the wind. Inside my trousers I was wearing pyjamas and inside my shoes two pairs of socks. My heavy German tweed coat with its woollen lining was doing its heavy German work. I was cold at the extremities but I made it in three-quarters of an hour, and no frostbite. So it can be done – that's not the problem. It's only that I wonder should one go to the office every day, weekends included? Or rather, should one *want* to? What's the attraction? I'm suspicious of that voluptuous filing cabinet, with its see-through drawer, its key-hole opening upon the Snow-White Goddess. Have I ever been to Denmark? Did I ever know a bourgeois lady called Bodil who danced like a demon and refused to kiss me in the snow? Was it part of something dreamed last night (when I woke and couldn't remember the geography of my apartment) or am I right in recalling someone telling me that Ashtree's itinerary will take him to Scandinavia?

Strange things happen in strange lands. One of the movies I shared inadvertently with Ms Libby Valtraute was by Pasolini. It was called *Theorem*. A beautiful young man comes into a middle-class household – mother father son daughter and maid. Beautiful young man is Christ – or at least I think that's the intention. Each member of the household becomes obsessed with him, and they all respond to him sexually because (I'm guessing at what Maestro Pasolini intended) that's the only way we, the modern decadent bourgeoisie, have of responding to anything. And isn't it true? Ms Valtraute's fur collar in the half light of the movie house has set me thinking of Danish Bodil whom I hugged (or was it Ashtree hugged her?) in the snow, and who might have said to Jesus Christ disguised as a beautiful young man, 'I am very hot-blooded. If I kiss you I will get excited.' Then a boy with an angel face (continuing Pasolini's movie) runs in flapping his arms and bearing a telegram calling the beautiful young man away. The young man goes. The whole family is bereft and each goes mad in a different way. The most successful is the maid because she still has the vehicle of primitive Catholicism. She returns to the village, sits out of doors, refuses all food but boiled nettles (why boil them – I mean why not go the whole hog?), cures a sick boy, levitates above the rooftops (a good job there by the special effects team), and finally has herself buried alive on a muddy building site at dawn.

At the interval I watch Ms Valtraute's fur collar but it sits facing forward and doesn't move. It's possible (anything is possible) she has vacated it. Round two is a French movie by Resnais, *Mon Oncle Americain*. I saw it in London two years ago but I was suffering jet lag and fell asleep. It portrays three lives which intersect, and the narrative, documentary style, is cut into by a 'scientific' account of human behaviour in terms which mix Skinnerian behaviourism and Freudian psychology. It seems to me affectionate, tolerant ('It is Tone that makes Music' used to be the motto of my old school) but on some point of sexual politics Resnais may well have erred. When the lights go up Ms Valtraute and her fur collar are nowhere to be seen.

Back in my apartment I'm getting ready for my big empty bed when the fire alarm sounds. I remain very calm, reading the instructions on the back of the door. They tell me I should remain very calm. I should inch the door open. If there's flame out there I should close it again. Go for the balcony. (I'm on the twelfth floor – twelve out of 34 – and I remember someone saying the longest ladders would only go up eleven floors.) If there are no flames and not too much smoke I should proceed groundward by the stairway. Don't use the lift. I put on shoes, take my big coat and scarf, toque – but no, why not die in style? I put on the Helmet Schmidt cap and make my way to the stairs. There are no flames, no smoke, just the clanging of bells, deafening, impossible to ignore, and a lot of people, increasing in number as I work my way down. Walking to the university in daylight on a Sunday it seemed Quinton had been vacated of its population – all but two or three of us, unwitting survivors, who had missed news of the evacuation or survived the neutron bomb. But why should anyone come out? Outside of working hours a North American city in winter is a lot of people watching television. Here they come now, down the stairs, wearing anything from nightdress to battledress. We gather in the foyer. The firetruck arrives. Someone on the eighth has set a kitchen alight. It's soon out, but down in the foyer we're getting to know one another. Beer cans arrive, and more beer cans. Someone has a tape deck, a regular ghettoblaster up on the railing of the mezzanine, and soon we're all drinking and dancing, the flashing red and orange lights of the firetruck turning the lobby into a disco. This is Locomotion again. Oh hot-blooded Bodil! Oh chilly Ms Valtraute! Where are your furry collars? Where are your sexual politics? Lonely and tearful, happy to be clasped to Melancholy's incomparable bosom, the Distinguished Visitor dances solo among the beer cans in the flashing lights of Quinton's largest firetruck.

20

Seen from the outside the Hubert Harrison-Jones Memorial Building in which Ashtree's office is situated is anonymous, dull brown, executing a quarter turn to imitate a bend in the river, so all its rooms along one side look down that wooded slope to the ice. Inside, it's all white stucco, glass and open spaces, with cloth banners in orange, green and gold hanging down through two and three floors of a central open area and catching the afternoon sunlight.

I sit at Alban Ashtree's desk reading a poem sequence by Alban Ashtree. Maybe he sat here writing it. It's about Death and the Snow Maiden. He longs for Death. He longs for the Snow Maiden. I keep looking up from the poem and down through the trees below the window. The shadows appear curiously blue across the clean white surface. Through the trees comes a tall shapely figure. She pauses at the top of the slope to regain breath, pulling off her toque and shaking out a shower of red-gold hemp. She looks up at this window and I wave nervously down to her. She smiles a sort of inward acknowledgement – not exactly a rebuff, but there's no return of my wave, and in a moment she's skimming away out of sight, around towards the main entrance.

I turn to the poems submitted for tonight's Creative Writing session. It occurs to me that some of them contain Snow Maidens and others Divine Derelicts. The Ashtree, it seems, casts a long shadow. The sun's still shining and I go out trying to find a trail that's firmly trodden down to the river. After twenty minutes I'm on the bank, the ice stretching away up-river and down, with drifts of snow heaped on it. I want to walk on it, never having walked on water, and I'm sure it would be safe. There are ski-tracks across it; and someone has told me the ice is two or three feet thick. But there's no one about, I've seen that trail of thaw where warm water spills from the power station up-river, I know my optimism where water is concerned often leads me into error (is Ms Valtraute an Aquarian?), and I can imagine how quickly the heavy German tweed would go down. One Distinguished Visitor, vanished without trace. So I content myself with a long look and two photographs. By the time I've found my way back up the slope my legs feel deeply chilled and my face is burning.

The phone rings. It's Dan Dugan wanting to talk about the submissions for tonight's Creative Writing class, and warning me to go easy on Ms Hanratty who's under sedation for an unhappy affair. I promise all due care and caution with Ms Hanratty. My eyes go around the room while we talk over the poems submitted, and I notice drawer number three with its few millimetres overlap. I wonder about calling Mrs Merrill in to unlock the cabinet and relock it with drawer three in place, but that nervous urgency has gone from the thought and I decide, 'Not yet.'

In my apartment this weekend, devising diversions and exercises for myself, I did some jogging. The apartment is large, but not large enough. I ran I think it was 50 times from the entrance to the sliding doors that open on to the balcony, then past the television set into the bedroom, around and across the double bed, back through the living room to the door again. Then I got more adventurous and extended my run out of the apartment into the vestibule, or lobby, or whatever that space out there's called. The building is circular, you understand, with elevators running up the middle. When you step out of an elevator you're at the still centre, with green carpet (green on this floor – different colours for different floors) – longer haired, but matching the apartment in colour, and running off the floors and up the walls, I suppose for insulation against noise. Encircling this central space runs the corridor off which the apartments open. So I listened out for the bells that would warn me if the lift was stopping at my floor and included that circular corridor in my run. It made for some fine turns of speed, and a little excitement.

And in the library on Saturday afternoon I found a copy of a New Zealand literary magazine. It was called *Landslide*, and there was a story about two young men on motorbikes riding through the long green-haired countryside south of Auckland. An *Easy Rider* kind of story – one of those up-to-the-minute fictions by writers who deny themselves every little gem of coincidence or connection turned over in the path of their wandering furrow. The two young men on motorbikes are returning home to a farm in the Bay of Plenty where a girl, who is sister of one and the former lover of the other, is expecting them. She, however, is now engaged to marry another man. In a pub along the way they're goaded by a bully into a fight and one of the two smashes a bottle over the head of their tormentor. They vanish into the night and ride away on their powerful bikes leaving they don't know what, but maybe a corpse, behind. And of course that's all about that. There's no connection with what happens next, no thread to be taken up later, because this is life, man. A slice of life. No phoney plot. No circular corridor bringing you back where you started.

Reading it I translated it into a Western movie. Two cowboys ride into a town on their way home after a long absence. In a saloon someone picks a fight with them, and our hero – former lover of the waiting girl – is called. He's reluctant, of course, but fast (yep), and when the bad guy draws he shoots him dead. They sink their whiskies and ride on out of town. They return to the beautiful girl on the ranch, and soon she's falling in love again with our hero, whose presence makes her recognise she hasn't ever loved the man she's engaged to marry. But then comes the word that her fiancé has been shot dead in a saloon gunfight and that the killer and his friend rode away into the night.

Now write on . . .

My first public lecture as Distinguished Visitor is called 'What is the Modern and Where did it Go?' Everyone likes the title, but in the course of delivering it I stray away from my prepared script and begin to talk about Ashtree's poems; and I wind up with a quotation from one of his unpublished notebooks, one of many memorable remarks of his I've found and jotted down on scraps of paper which tend to present themselves at unplanned moments, in manila folders, in pockets, among papers on my desk, or just in memory, taking me by surprise all over again. 'To be perfectly lucid,' the quotation goes, 'is to deprive yourself of mystery and your reader of that sense of effort and discovery necessary to high art.'

Chairman Hyde is silent as we walk away from the lecture theatre. We're joined by Dan Dugan, Eugene Fish, and one or two others. The talk is desultory and general. Have I caused offence? We drink coffee in the Faculty Club, and Eugene Fish tells a story about a gay tourist who goes on a world cruise. He finishes up at the Vatican watching the Pope officiating at some ceremony or public mass, swinging a smoky censer. 'I love his drag,' the tourist says to the lady standing next to him; 'but I think his handbag's on fire.'

Back in my office I take down Ashtree's poems again and read here and there, trying to remember what I said about them and to guess where in my remarks I went wrong. And then a small fist knocks at the door and it's a fur collar standing there surrounding the beautiful freckled blue-eyed face of Ms Valtraute. Has she come to say something nice about my lecture? Not exactly. But she asks could we talk some time about sexual politics in Commonwealth poets. She thinks I may be able to help her make her selection. I pretend to consult a crowded timetable before suggesting tomorrow at 4 pm. 'Let's go for a beer,' she says, 'so it will be business and pleasure.' 'I look forward to it,' I say truthfully.

A minute later there's another knock. Bob Wilcox, who has the office next to mine, is inviting me to eat pizzas with him and his teenage daughter and his daughter's friend who is from Mexico. I throw Ashtree into my bag and follow Bob down to the carpark. At the pizza place the two girls talk Spanish and play records while Bob and I talk about French Canada, and Margaret Trudeau having sex in a car with Jack Nicholson, and Commonwealth Literature, and finally about Alban Ashtree. Bob wasn't there to hear my lecture, so I explain how I drifted on to the subject of Ashtree's poetry, and then felt uncertain what people thought of the lecture. 'Well I guess,' Bob Wilcox says, 'they don't like him.' 'You mean his work? They don't admire it?' 'Oh his work's okay,' Bob says. 'It's *him* they don't like.'

On the way back from the pizza place Bob gives some friends a lift. Daughter Monica climbs on my knee to make room for them, and for a few minutes I have hair in my face and my arms around a teenage daughter.

Other casual entries in Ashtree's notebooks read: 'I am too much given to doing my duty'; and 'Writing is a poor substitute for Sex. But so is everything except Sex.'

It seems clear that the moment Bodil refused Ashtree's request to let him kiss her in the street outside the disco, she regretted it. Next day they met by chance in the city Art Gallery and, being an honest and direct Scandinavian lady, she told him of the fact. He suggested he kiss her at once, behind a large piece of sculpture, but she had something more thorough-going in mind. What's not clear is why they didn't use Ashtree's hotel room. Of course it may have been some bizarre preference. But Ashtree's record seems plain enough.

25

That night the big German Ford was parked on the edge of a ploughed field outside the town with its windows up, its seats down, its engine running and its heater working. And while snow drifted down, Ashtree discovered (his notes are graphically particular) what a respectable Danish bourgeois lady had meant when she said, 'If I kiss you I get excited.'

And another aphorism from the cabinet: 'The generation of writers before mine suffered the pain of going unread because they were Canadian. Mine lives with the indignity of being read only for that reason.'

And a postscript: 'Most of the bastards live with it without discomfort.'

The forecasters have been predicting that some high-level meeting of contrary streams of air somewhere over the Rockies will 'send the temperatures soaring towards zero', but I've seen no sign of it. The bus strike, long threatened, has begun, and I walk to Quinton University across the high-level bridge wearing pyjamas and extra socks under my trousers and on my head the toques, the one with the mask under the other. Where is the Helmet Schmidt look? The little cap of wapiti suede lies crushed and defeated at the bottom of my bag. Below the bridge I can see skiers on trails through the trees that cover the slopes down to the river. In a school playground the children rocket down an ice-slide into a bank of snow. A hot-air balloon floats over the city. A bookshop has a display of the work of a Canadian woman poet who killed herself in Quinton three or four days ago. (If they'd had the display last week, would she still be alive?)

In Ashtree's office I discuss the novels of Iris Murdoch with a PhD student who is writing a thesis on them. He's a Kurd from Iraq, and he plans, before returning home, to buy an apartment in Vienna where he will spend his summers listening to European music. I read the poems offered me by a sessional from Bombay. They are full of fine old flourishes, as if the English language had been set aside these past seventy years, and taken up fresh out of the cooler. I take a class on 'The Waste Land' for which I receive a round of applause. At 4 pm I keep my appointment with Ms Valtraute. We drink beer under the drab rafters of the Graduates Club, and talk about Henry Miller, Norman Mailer, and her childhood on a farm in Saskatchewan. The farmhouse had no electricity and no central heating. It was heated by a furnace in the kitchen. In Libby's bedroom upstairs icicles hung from nails in the wall, frost formed on the inside panes of her windows, and the water in the glass by her bed was frozen over by morning. Until she was twenty she never saw a tree taller than eight feet. She was twenty-three when she first saw the sea – the age (I tell her) at which I first saw snow. I don't tell her how far life has taken me into my forties before showing me my first frozen river.

As for Miller and Mailer – she may be more relaxed over her beer but she's not prepared to sign an armistice in the war of the sexes, or even discuss the possibility of a SALT treaty. Miller is a sexist for whom women are objects. Mailer has a macho hangup. I tell her Miller seems to me to love women above all else in life. 'He loves to fuck them,' she says, with wintry Saskatchewan candour. We call a cab and cross the river to the town side, a Japanese restaurant where a Japanese cook in a tall white hat prepares a meal for a dozen people grouped around a table which adjoins his large electric hot-plate. It's a curious combination of East and West, like those Western-style popular songs sung in Japanese and intended to be orientally occidental but better described (it's my little joke for Libby Valtraute) as accidentally disorientated. We get a lucky number with our meal and Libby's wins third prize, a little Japanese vase, mine no prize, but I'm given a pair of chopsticks.

The meal has been large, enjoyable if unremarkable, and the sake has loosened us a little. I suggest coffee at my apartment which is only a couple of blocks away, and I notice the predictable pattern of all this, and the fact that, feminism or not, I'm permitted to pay the bill. The coffee is instant – all I have; but we turn the lights down low (my green-haired apartment has of course a dimmer-switch) and look out at the city towers glittering in the icy air, and the broad white wandering ice-path of the river under the moonlight. I sit beside Libby on the same couch, and now and then our knees touch. When she says she should maybe call a cab I suggest another cup of coffee and she agrees so readily, I'm almost disappointed. Won't her feminism assert itself? Has she no principles? Or is this just a big Man Trap leading to the Saskatchewan fist in my Pacific mouth the moment I make the first move? When, close to 1 a.m. she says again she must call a cab, I don't object. She lifts the instrument, begins punching the numbers with her beautiful strong prairie index, then stops. 'This is silly,' she says. 'I want to go to bed with you.'

The spirit of Mailer, macho man, takes a dive off the balcony, twelve floors onto the icy pavement, and dies. The ghost of Miller is already in the next room, not so much turning back the covers as performing the dance of the seven veils with them. Is this feminism? Why resist the flow of history, especially when it offers to irrigate the desert?

My second public lecture, a week after the first, is called 'Modernism – an art of fragments', and it goes much better than the first because I stick to my script and resist the temptation to get on to the subject of Alban Ashtree. At question time an elderly academic expresses doubts about whether there can be an art of fragments. 'Fragments are fragments,' he says. 'And art is art.' My reply includes references to Picasso and Braque, Pasolini and Resnais,

Stravinsky and Berg, and of course something about the flow of history, and the pointlessness of setting your face against it. As I say this my eyes wander over the audience towards Libby Valtraute who is inconspicuously placed at the back near the door. I haven't seen her today, though I've been conscious of her in bed with me during the night. She has in the past few days taken possession of the spare key to my apartment and she comes and goes according to whim, or some schedule of her own, often creeping in after I've gone to sleep and leaving early before I wake. Only her fat-free yoghurt in the refrigerator, her lemon-and-honey soap in the bath, and her red-gold hempen hair around the plug hole, reassure me that she's not a figment or an invention. But though I'm certain of her reality and of her occasional presence in my bed, I can't be sure whether it's an accurate memory or a deluding dream I carry about with me, of waking in the middle of the night to find her cradling my head against her naked breasts and weeping silently into my hair, murmuring a word I can't catch, but which puts vaguely into my sleep-fuddled brain the thought of a breakfast cereal.

Two hours after it's over I come into the Faculty Club and half a dozen of the Comp Lit Department are discussing my lecture. There's an awkward silence until Eugene Fish explains to me that they've been talking about my resemblance to Alban Ashtree. They've remarked on it before, and on the coincidence that I should be occupying his room. And today I've done something with my glasses while answering a question which was, they assure me, 'pure Alban'. Eugene does an imitation of it. But that dark part of my brain is listening to Ashtree's forename, Alban, as they pronounce it. And that breakfast cereal thought of in the night – wasn't it All Bran? Is it possible that what I've woken to hear Libby Valtraute whimpering as she wept into my hair was Ashtree's name?

The high-level meeting of air-streams with its consequent thaw comes and goes too rapidly to change anything. For half a day the icy snow turns to slush in the streets and begins to run away into gutters, but that night it all turns to ice again and in the morning fresh snow has fallen. Bob Wilcox has the afternoon off and finds gear for me so we can go cross-country skiing. We take a trail down to the river and cross the ice to follow another trail along the riverbank for an hour or more until it brings us to a lodge where there's a fire and hot drinks. It's late when we get back and in the Faculty Club there's a tense atmosphere. Eugene Fish tries to say something but stutters to a halt. Chairman Hyde assumes the mantle of his office and delivers it straight. The department has had a telegram this afternoon. It's about Ashtree. Not good news. Bad in fact. The worst. Yes, he's afraid so. A grievous loss. Ashtree died in an avalanche yesterday, climbing somewhere in the Austrian Alps.

I lie awake in my overheated apartment wondering what it would be like to die under an avalanche of snow. It seems gentle soft stuff and I'm so unfamiliar with its ways I can't imagine it as a violent death. I'm drifting towards and away from sleep, asking myself could anyone be called Alban Ashtree and die so alliterative a death – in an avalanche in the Austrian Alps? Are there Alps in Austria? Or, on the other hand, if it's all real and true, could it really be an accident? Has Ashtree designed a picturesque end for himself?

I get up and phone Libby Valtraute again but there's still no answer. I slide back both panes of the little half window that opens from my bedroom on to the balcony, and for a few moments the cold blast is refreshing, but soon it's too cold and I close one pane leaving the other half open. Out there the moon is shining on the snow that has heaped and frozen in layers on the unused balcony. I wonder where Libby has been since the news came of Ashtree's death. I have his latest book of poems by my bed and I open it and read the lines

> Idea of a river was harder than
> the river itself while the winged
> mercury fell through the floors
> through ice through
> layers of sleep that were a kind of death.

His reputation has been growing in recent years – everyone seems agreed on that, and chairman Hyde has said that there will be Canada Council money for whoever gets the job of editing his collected works.

I pull the sheet over me and turn off the light. From this angle the big white moon appears balanced on the balcony rail. My eyes flicker towards sleep again and the moon's face is the face of Libby Valtraute. 'Alban,' she weeps. 'Alban.'

My Snow Maiden! My Snow-White Goddess!

Class, Race, Gender:
a Post-Colonial Yarn

IT WILL PERHAPS SERVE A DISARMING PURPOSE AND MAKE what I have to record seem less serious than it is, or than it ought to be, if I begin by explaining that this is a story told by Bertie to Billy, who told it to me. More recently Bertie told me the story himself, so I've heard it twice and have had the chance to ask questions and fill gaps that remained after the first hearing.

I got to know Bertie and Billy a long time ago when we were all students in England. Bertie was, and indeed is and will always be even when he's dead, an Englishman. His fuller, though not entire (there are several intermediate ones) name is Herbert Lawson-Grieve. Friends and family called him Bertie, and so, although we, Billy and I, found it absurd, adding to the general feeling that he was less a real person than a character out of P. G. Wodehouse, Bertie is what we called him.

Billy is South African. His full name is Villiers de Groot Graaf which among our group became Billy Goat Gruff – Billy for short. Billy and Bertie were friends before I knew them. They were at Oxford together, at the same College, Merton, Billy studying ('reading', as they say in England) engineering, Bertie law. Like Bertie, Billy had money, lots of it, which came from what he called 'a family in diamonds'.

I was a graduate student on a scholarship from New Zealand, writing a thesis which I hoped might be published as a book. But it was our passion for sport that brought us together – that, and a particular kind of boyish temperament. ('Chappish', I think it would be called these days, with, of course, deep disapproval.) There was a lot of beer drinking, a lot of horsing about, a lot of talk about 'girls'. We loved Western movies and practised shoot-outs in the parks. I think we were quite serious students, but we were having a good time.

There was another student of that time I should mention because he has provided my title – or the first half of it: Peter Mapplethwaite from Scunthorpe. I've once or twice glanced at a map looking for Scunthorpe and not succeeded in finding it, but the way Pete pronounced it, and the word itself, suggested slums, coal mines, sunless skies and rickets – the part of England which those of us who were (shallow and ignorant, no doubt) visitors skirted around on our way to the lakes or the moors, to North Wales or to Scotland.

Mapplethwaite was a Marxist and a man of the people. Peoplethwaite, Bertie called him; and then Marplethorpe, Pepperpot, Maxiwank, Whistlestop, Cuttlefish – anything at all but his real name. Pete could be good company. Billy and I imitated his accent and he imitated ours. He knew me as the New Zillander who liked igg sendwiches; and Billy as the Seth Ufrican who didn't want to talk about bleck prytest.

Pete had absolutely no sense of tune, but he sang dialect songs – I suppose they were from his region – in a flat ugly-funny voice. Some of these took the form of dialogues, one of which went, as I remember,

> 'Where's tha bin, lud?'
> ''awkeen paypers.'
> ' 'o for?'
> 'Meyuncle Benjamin.'

'Wha's 'e gin thee?'
'Skinny ole 'et'ny.'
'Silly ole blawk
'e ought ta dee.'

I tried to make Pete part of the group but it was no use. It didn't matter too much that he sometimes wanted to lecture Billy about the situation of the 'blecks'. There were a few occasions when Billy hung his head in helpless shame, and then flared up in angry Boer pride; but mostly he could cope with it. But it was the two Englishmen, Pete and Bertie, who couldn't mix. It wasn't even that there was great animosity between them. It seemed more like embarrassment.

Once I asked Bertie was it a problem for him that Mapplethwaite was a Marxist. Lord no, he said; that was no problem at all. Lots of chaps from school (he always spoke of 'school' as if the word meant to me exactly what it meant to him) had been Lefties. I waited for him to go on and for a moment he seemed flummoxed. Then he lowered his voice and said that for him, personally, the problem was Mapplethwaite's feet.

I thought at first that this was some kind of joke, but it wasn't. We'd all been at a party in north Oxford when Pete had vomited and passed out cold – so 'cold' we thought he was dead. We'd got him on to a bed and someone had taken off his shoes and socks.

'He had such nasty long white monkey-feet,' Bertie said, almost in awe; 'and the soles – did you notice? – they were *black*.'

Those feet, and Bertie's reaction to them, belonged to something peculiarly and impenetrably English, and I gave up my efforts towards an accommodation. I didn't want to seem a busybody on someone else's turf. But I've gone on seeing Pete on my visits to England, calling on him at the north London Polytechnic where he lectures on what's called Culture and

Gender Studies, and going for a drink with him at his local.

Over the years Pete has been a Moscow communist, then a Peking communist, his faith coming to rest finally, when Mao died and the Gang of Four were arrested, on the régime in Albania. Later again, when the Berlin Wall came down and piece by piece the whole communist empire fell apart, I expected to find him depressed and defeated, but he wasn't. On my last visit he seemed more relaxed and confident than he'd been for years. Communism was pure now, pure theory; it hadn't yet, he explained, been put into practice – not anywhere. All those attempts at it had been corrupt and imperfect. Communism lay somewhere up ahead, the great future which all the world's peoples would enjoy when at last they came to their senses and realized the evils of capitalism. Meanwhile all serious 'analysis' (his favourite word) of anything and everything came down to three words: class, race and gender.

That's why Peter Mapplethwaite figures in my account: because if I told him this story (something I can't imagine I would want to do) he would say that it illustrates perfectly the justness of the intellectual framework which has ruled his life; whereas to me it illustrates (if it illustrates anything) just the opposite – that life is subtler and more complex than the theories men construct to explain it.

I've also continued to see Bertie – much more of him than of Pete – and so has Billy. But Billy's visits to England and mine have never coincided; and it wasn't until he came to New Zealand, accompanying the Springboks on their first post-Apartheid tour, that we were able to get together again. Our talk was of rugby, of the new South Africa (which made him proud, but nervous too), and of the old days when we'd been students in England. Bertie's name came up often, and we were sorry he wasn't there – but we knew he would be watching the test matches on television; and I had an amusing and, as Pete would have said, culturally insensitive fax from him when a South African forward bit the All Blacks captain's ear and was caught by the cameras.

'Anent ear-eating,' Bertie's message ran. 'Why the fuss? When in Rome, n'est ce pas?'

What did he mean? What could he have meant except that cannibalism was a local tradition, wasn't it – so why not?

From time to time Billy and I have each tried to persuade Bertie to visit us at home. His answer to Billy has always been that he would come 'when South Africa has a black President'. Since none of us believed this would happen in our lifetime, it was his way of saying he would never come. To my invitations he always replied (adopting what he thought was my accent), 'Tow far, moite. Thenks – oi'd love tow. But tow far.'

Bertie, of course, speaks that tortured, alternately clipped, squeezed, swallowed and diphthongised English which signals, even (and perhaps especially) to those who mock it, impeccable social credentials; and it is one of the jokes we share, and revert to often, that his second mother-in-law, who was French, could always understand my outlander's English but had the greatest difficulty making sense of his.

Bertie has lived most of his adult life in a beautiful house with a beautiful walled garden in the town of Marlow on the Thames. He inherited the place from a maiden great-aunt when he was still a young man; and for many years he commuted all the way in to London where he worked as a solicitor specialising in marine insurance which he liked to tell us was properly called 'bottomry'. After his third marriage Bertie gave up the City firm in which he'd risen to become a partner, and opened a small office of his own in his home town. He's there still, prosperous and apparently content, with a wife so young he sometimes jokingly introduces her as 'My wife and child'.

Bertie's house is full of sporting prints and cricketing

photographs. Along the hallways and up the stairs you can see the rugby and cricket teams – school, university, business and local – he has played for. There's a cabinet of sporting trophies, and pictures of two or three racehorses. I've noticed too that he's something of a Narcissus. There are several painted portraits of him around the house; and a rather grand gold-framed mirror in his dining room, placed where, when conversation around the table begins to run into the sand, he can pass the time staring at himself.

In the seventies Bertie let his hair grow rather long, with side-burns, and that's the look he has tended to stick with; and as the hair has thinned and gone grey-streaked, and fashions have changed, it has left him looking less than the dashing and fashionable fellow he once was. But he's tall (six foot two or three), strongly built, still handsome, still full of charm and energy and generosity. Bertie does things in style; and to be met by him at the station with flowers and champagne, as if you were a visiting foreign dignitary, is to experience a sort of expansiveness which none of us where I come from would be capable of, even if the wish and the impulse towards it should happen to stir.

It was when Billy was on one of his visits to England that Bertie told him the story about his involvement with the Cockney woman whose name was Thelma Button, but who was known to her workmates as Thelly, or sometimes Shell. During Billy's Springbok-accompanying visit to New Zealand he passed the story on to me. ('You're a writer, Carlo,' he said; 'you can disguise it can't you?') And so, on my most recent visit to England, when I recognised during a late night drinking session with Bertie that we were on the borders, so to speak, of this same narrative territory, I prompted, listened, questioned, remembered, reconstructed. Here is what I learned.

Bertie was, as he put it, 'between marriages at the time' –

depressed, bored, restless. This was in the last of his years working for the big impersonal City firm he'd been with for almost twenty years. His second wife, Françoise, had left him, not for another man, nor for any reason except that she'd grown to hate living in England. One day, with the help of the mother-in-law who couldn't understand Bertie's conversation, she packed her things and, with their child, returned to Paris.

'It was a fearsome blow to the pride,' Bertie said. 'Nothing like that had ever happened to me before. So of course the old mind went blank for a time and I came to consciousness a few months later realising I was drinking too much, eating fast fodder, not getting any exercise, becoming fat, ratty and inefficient. It was bad. All bad. That was when I started thinking about Shell.'

She served lunches in a popular place where lawyers often went for a quick bite when they weren't entertaining clients. She was small, well-shaped, bright-eyed, pretty, good-humoured, with the broadest of London accents, and she and Bertie had hit it off right from their first encounter. She teased him; he responded. Their exchanges were always (as he put it) 'remorselessly joky', but with an undertone of flirtation. But what really attracted him was her hair. It was shiny brown, wiry and curly, and despite her best efforts to keep it neat it sprang out from her head as if it had a life of its own. It was the kind of hair, he said, that you want desperately to touch.

Bertie never thought about this woman except when she was there in front of him, serving him salad or cottage pie. She was a very minor character in his life, one of thousands with walk-on parts. The idea that she might be more, or other, never occurred to him. When she disappeared from the lunch place and went to work somewhere else he didn't notice that she was gone.

Then one day he met her in the street. He was used to

seeing her in a white smock and apron, and if it hadn't been for that head of hair he might not have recognised her. She told him she had a new job, with hours that suited her better because she started early and was finished in time to pick up the kids (she had two, Jack and Jill) from school. Also she had every Wednesday afternoon free.

And then, taking him by surprise, she said if he was ever passing on a Wednesday afternoon he ought to drop in for a cuppa.

'It was the boldness of the thing,' Bertie said. 'You couldn't be mistaken about it. She just looked me in the eye, grinned wickedly, and said it. And then she wrote her address on a piece of paper and pushed it into my hand. I must have looked flabbergasted, but that only made her laugh. She said, "Come on Mister, don't look so frightened. Hasn't a pretty girl ever invited you to tea before?" And she walked off and left me there.'

Shortly after that Françoise, his lovely French wife, left him. There were those months of dereliction, and the realisation that he must take himself in hand, re-order his life, discipline himself. But it shouldn't, he told himself, be all hard work. There must be some fun, some entertainments, some good times. Clearing the pockets of a jacket and trousers one day, readying things for the dry cleaner, he found the slip of paper with Thelma Button's address, and remembered that invitation with its suggestion of a good deal more than tea.

So an affair (if that's the word for such an arrangement) started. Thelma, or Shelley as he was soon calling her, lived in a block of flats just off Clerkenwell Road near to Gray's Inn, only twenty minutes walk, or five by taxi, from Bertie's office which was close to the Barbican. His secretary learned to keep the hours from one to 3.30 clear on a Wednesday and he spent them in bed with Shelley; and even many years after what was to be their last dreadful encounter, Bertie couldn't speak of the first weeks and months of that association without a certain brightening of the eye and a lift in the voice.

The flat, on the second floor of a dingy red-brick apartment block, was drab and cramped, but it had a balcony looking inward to a shady courtyard with a single tree. They used to make love, then lie in bed looking out into the upper branches of the tree, talking, exchanging stories, dozing, until they'd recovered sufficiently to do it again, after which they would shower together and return to their separate lives.

Their talk was full of teasing and banter, but with a rich undertone of affection. He told her about the people in his office; she talked about Jack and Jill, family, neighbours. Because he called her Shelley he told her about the poet who had once lived in his town of Marlow, writing revolutionary poems while his wife Mary wrote *Frankenstein*. A week or so later she had *Frankenstein* beside her bed. She'd found it in a bookshop, bought it and read it. He asked what she thought of it.

''orrible,' she said. 'Did you like it Bertie?'

He had to admit he'd never read it.

Once he bought her a gold chain, knowing – or thinking – that she would have to hide it from her husband. But she made him help her put it on, saying she would never take it off.

'What about Arthur?' he asked. She said she would say she'd found it in the street.

Bertie seldom asked about Arthur, preferred not to hear or think about him; but now and then she would speak of him. He was a guard at the British Museum; and though she always said he was 'harmless', that was the best she could say of him. All day he sat in a chair watching over ancient vases and statues, and in the evening he sat watching television, especially football which didn't interest her in the least. His back was bad. He never had anything to say. Sometimes

Shelley would tell him about something she'd read or seen and he would say, 'That's very interesteen, Thel.' That's what he'd said when she told him the story of Frankenstein. 'Interesteen.' She seemed to find Arthur's pronunciation of that word unforgivable. It drove her mad. It excused her infidelity.

As Bertie explained it to me, it was some time before he began to understand what kind of a woman Thelma Button was and why she'd made him this, as it had seemed, outrageously frank offer of herself. She was not at all what he'd supposed – either 'wild', desperate, a beaten wife, or even attracted to him by his patrician looks and manner. Shelley was not inexperienced; but her life had been on the whole sober and orderly, constrained by modest beginnings, low income, early marriage, and two children born within a year of one another.

As for Bertie's attractions: she knew perfectly well that he was of a certain 'class'; but to her such men had always seemed faintly comic – not to be taken seriously. It was almost an obstacle to her liking him; just as her 'class' – the fact that she referred to her husband as 'Arfur', complained that her children came home 'filfy' from school, talked about someone having 'nuffing in 'is 'ead', or said she'd heard this or that 'on good aufori'y', had made her seem to Bertie quite beyond the pale. No. Bertie's attractiveness to her had been something else, something she herself found mysterious and inexplicable. All she could say about it was that it had something to do with his voice and his eyes and his laugh. And also, once she got to know him better, his smell. But almost from the first exchange between them she'd felt she was falling in love with him.

This was a fact which only slowly became clear to Bertie. He found it flattering, disconcerting, unintelligible, reassuring – both welcome and unwelcome; for while it made for great sex, and helped restore the confidence which a much-loved wife's departure had undermined, it also added a burden of responsibility and of guilt. Increasingly as he got to know Thelma Button, Bertie felt affection and gratitude. Her talk was lively and witty. Her generosity was boundless. Her body was lovely and her hair magical. He began to think of her as his secret garden. But to fall in love, even a little, with someone who had things 'on good aufori'y' was quite beyond him.

'Not possible,' he said when I asked him. 'Simply out of the question. Sometimes, you know, I'd try to imagine taking her to things – to dinner parties, Lord's, Wimbledon, Covent Garden. I'd try, Carlo. It was . . .' He looked at me with an expression that appealed for understanding, for absolution. 'It was unthinkable.'

So he decided he must stop seeing her. If she'd been able to take their affair as he did, as an adventure, a diversion, an unlooked for luxury, a secret bonus Life had handed out with no strings or complications, there would have been no problem. But he could see that every visit made the love she felt for him, and which he couldn't think of matching, more powerful, more all-consuming.

She, of course, soon recognised that the depth of her feeling troubled him, and she tried to conceal it or make light of it. But there were moments when she would say, 'I'd die for you, Bertie,' or even (and much worse), 'I'd let you kill me if you wanted to. I'd love you for it.' He would be struck with a sense of awe and helplessness then, and with the wish to escape. To have evoked great love could only be good for his wounded ego; on the other hand, to find himself unable to return it inevitably reduced the beneficial effect. Herbert Lawson-Grieve's secret garden had begun to have about it the feel of a cage.

But still the decision that he must end their affair wasn't translated into action. He would think of it as he left her flat, resolving that this visit would be the last. By the following

Monday the resolve would be gone. By Wednesday he would hardly be able to complete his morning's work for thinking of what the afternoon was to bring. But now, because he was in two minds about Shelley, a sort of ambiguity had begun to creep into his feelings about what he did with her in bed. He enjoyed – enjoyed enormously – and yet did not enjoy. He marvelled, and was half-repelled. Sometimes he felt like a circus animal required to do ever-more remarkable tricks. Shelley was the trainer and her whip was true love.

The break didn't come until he was sent to New York on business for the firm. It wasn't a city he enjoyed and he would normally have asked them to send someone else. This time he accepted the task willingly, and even made it last longer than was necessary. By the time he got back to London he felt the Shelley habit had been broken.

But now came phone calls from her; and when these were blocked off by his secretary, there was a postcard. It was of a large pink breast painted to look like a winking pig, the nipple its snout. On the back she had written, 'Here's my knocker, Bertie luv. Where's yours?'

This, coming to him in the office, giggled over by the secretaries, was outrageous – but of course she meant it to be. Bertie was angry, but he was also ashamed. He had tried to end the affair because she loved him too much, and that seemed to him the honourable thing to do; but it had not been honourable – it had been cowardly and wrong – to try to end it by simply absenting himself without a word. He must go and (as he put it) 'face the music'.

The 'music', however, when it came on the following Wednesday was not a simple and catchy tune. At first, when he tried to tell her they must call it off, she reproached him – something she hadn't done before; then she wept, shouted, told him she would always love him, threatened suicide, insulted him. He found it painful, and the pain focused especially on one fact – that she appeared to have dressed her-self up for the encounter, and that the clothes seemed to him in the worst possible taste.

As Bertie explained it to me, he has no exact memory for women's clothes, often doesn't remember colours, or remembers them incorrectly – yet at the same time he always takes away a generalised, and in some ways quite precise, impression. Shelley, as he remembered her that day, was wearing a yellow dress of some kind of stiff material, with a short skirt, and around her head, over that rebellious but briefly tamed hair, a band of the same colour.

'There seemed to be little bows and frills everywhere,' he said. 'I may be exaggerating, but it seemed to me she only needed a tray of sweets and ices and she could have gone to a fancy dress ball as an old-fashioned cinema usherette.'

He had never, he told me, felt so fond of her, nor so self-reproachful and so determined to protect her. He couldn't give her what she wanted – he could not; and so the only thing for it was to remove himself. That's what he tried to explain, while she argued, wept, threatened, pleaded.

At last however, when he was on the point of exhaustion, despair and rage, she changed tack – seemed to accept that he was going, and that he wouldn't be back. Before he went, however, she would like, she said, to show him her 'new friend'. She went to the drawer beside her bed and took something out. He thought it must be a photograph, but what she held up to him was a plastic vibrator. Bertie knew what it was, but only because there had once been an Anne Summers sex shop in Tottenham Court Road and from time to time he'd looked in as he went by and had seen such things, all manner of phallic shapes and sizes, on shelves in long rows.

She held it out for him to touch, but he drew back from it. She pressed a little switch and it began to buzz. She put one foot on the bed and he saw that she was wearing no underclothes. She ran the plastic head of the buzzing phallus through her pubic hair, which grew as coarse and curly as the hair on her head. And then, while he watched, slowly, very slowly, she pushed it into herself.

'My mouth went suddenly dry,' Bertie said, 'and I knew it – I was done for. I said, "I'm going, Shelley" and she said – putting her head back, you know, as though she was really enjoying it – "You're not going nowhere, my Ber'ie." She was right of course. I felt as if I was going towards the door but I wasn't. She was like a magnet. It was like being dragged bodily, against your will.'

He'd been looking down into his drink as he told me this, and I remember how he looked up now, appealing for a friend's compassion. 'You have to understand, Carlo, I was hungry for it. I'd been all those weeks in New York, and there'd been nothing. Nothing but the occasional hand-job.'

'So,' I said, when he fell silent. 'What did you do?'

It was a silly question. 'What do you think I did?' he replied. 'I took it out and put mine in. We did it dressed, half-dressed, undressed. We did it up against the wall, on the floor, in the bed. We did it standing, sitting, lying. I didn't care any more. Fuck it, I thought. Life's too difficult. Let's just enjoy ourselves. And that's what we did. Three o'clock came around, 3.30 – I didn't care. I was busy. I was fucking. I was happy. I was being myself for a change and I was enjoying it.'

So the afternoon passed. And it occurred to him afterwards that she must all along have been confident of success, because she'd arranged for Jack and Jill to go to a friend's place for supper. They fucked and they talked, and talked and fucked, and finally they slept . . .

Bertie was woken by her shaking him, staring down at him. 'Wake up,' she was saying. 'Jesus Christ, Ber'ie, wake fucking *up*. It's *'im*! It's *Arfur*!'

Then she was out of bed and across the room to the hallway. He heard her snib the Yale lock. There was a conversation going on in the corridor – Arthur talking to a neighbour. In a moment he would try to open his own door with the key, and find he couldn't.

Back in the bedroom Shelley was gathering up her things. She hissed at Bertie to get dressed. ''e'll go downstairs to the caretaker to report there's something wrong with the lock. Then you scarpa. Go down the other stairs. I'll pretend I snibbed it by mistake.'

She vanished into the bathroom. And now from the front door came the scraping of Arthur's key as he tried to turn it in the lock. Bertie dragged on his underpants and trousers, wrestled with his shirt which he found had lost a button in the earlier, equally violent, struggle to get it off.

Arthur's voice came through the door. 'Thel? You in there Thelma?' He rattled the door handle. 'Thel?'

And then the key was withdrawn, the voice muttered to itself, footsteps receded down the corridor.

Now, Bertie thought – now was his chance to escape. He would get out and would never come back. He thought of setting off, running, carrying his shoes. But no, the idea was ridiculous. Some sort of dignity had to be preserved.

He was sitting on the bed's edge dragging on his socks when he heard a new sound, a scraping and scrambling. The balcony out there was shared with the flat next door. Arthur had gone through the flat of the neighbour he'd been talking to in the corridor. Now, from the balcony, he was scrambling up over a closed window to an open fanlight.

From where Bertie sat he could see, across the hallway and through another door, a pair of long black-trousered legs pushing, sliding, hanging, dropping.

There was a thump as two feet hit the sitting room floor. Shelley's voice quavered from the bathroom. 'That you, Arfur?'

Bertie put his head down and dragged at his shoes. He tugged at the laces. Footsteps approached. At that moment, he told me, he felt a desperate calm. The blow would come down on the back of his head, on his neck – he had no doubt of that. He wouldn't defend himself; couldn't. He would die; but it wasn't fear he felt – it was embarrassment. It was shame.

Two large black shiny guard's shoes arrived and planted themselves opposite the two brown shoes into which Bertie's feet were still refusing to fit. He persisted, dragging the laces wide apart.

'One has to do something while waiting to die,' Bertie said. 'I remember wondering would the blow hurt, or would I pass instantly and painlessly into another world of floating shapes saying things like, "Hullo, dear. I'm your mother."'

But there was no blow. Nothing was said. There was only the heavy breathing of a wronged husband who had just climbed through a fanlight.

'I raised my eyes slowly.' (Bertie was acting it out for me now – bending forward, twisting his head around to look up at the occupant of those shiny shoes.) 'There was the line of the trousers. When I got to the thighs I saw the hands, hanging at his sides. They were coffee coloured, with sickly palms. I raised my eyes further and there was a coffee face to match. My first thought was, "Why the fuck did she never tell me he was black?"'

The dark mask looking down at him showed no violence. That ought to have been a relief; but violence would have been simpler. It would have given him something to do.

He tried to read Arthur's face. There was anxiety in the eyes; and around the mouth something like contempt.

'This is a dreadful business,' Bertie managed to say. 'I'm really most frightfully sorry.'

He stood, picking his jacket up from the floor. That uncovered the vibrator. They both, he and black Arthur, looked down at it lying there like a severed penis.

Bertie said he'd better go.

Shelley had been right – Arthur wasn't a talker; but his silence at this moment seemed strangely powerful and impressive.

Bertie moved out into the hall. His walk was unsteady. At the bathroom door he stopped and called to Shelley that he was going.

The bolt slid back and she appeared in a dressing gown. Behind her he could see the yellow dress trampled on the wet tiled floor. She nodded to him, glanced at Arthur.

Bertie moved to the front door – only a step or two in those cramped quarters. He unsnibbed the lock, opened the door, and felt a moment of relief.

But was it right to leave without another word? He turned. Shelley had come out of the bathroom, Arthur out of the bedroom, and they were standing side by side, 'like two piano keys,' Bertie said, 'the ebony and the ivory. They made a handsome couple.'

To Arthur Bertie said, 'You won't hurt her.' He meant it to be something midway between a question and an instruction.

Arthur said, 'Out.' That was the beginning and the end of his talk.

Shelley looked at Bertie reassuringly. She was quite safe seemed to be the message. So he went, closing the door gently behind him.

Out in the street he was assailed all over again by embarrassment. He turned west, away from his office, crossed Gray's Inn Road, walked along to Southampton Row. In Kingsway there was a men's clothes shop that had always, as long as he could remember, announced that it was having a Closing Down Sale. He went in and chose himself an unpleasant business shirt that had a faint green tinge to it. It would replace the one with the tear and the hanging button.

He also thought of it as a penance. Handing over his credit card he asked the young woman did she have any with hair linings.

'So-rree?' she quacked at him. He didn't repeat it.

It was raining now. He took a taxi back to the office. The secretaries had gone. He sat at his desk looking out at the rain drifting past the ugly looming towers of the Barbican. He thought of Françoise and a few tears sprang into his eyes – a mixture of anger and regret. He thought of Arthur's shiny black shoes and winced. He heard the partner in the next office getting ready to leave. He went to her door. Her name was Coral Strand. They'd worked together for years, knew one another well.

'That's a nasty shirt, Herbert,' she said at once. 'It's not the one you had on this morning.'

He never got used to the fact that women noticed clothing so precisely. 'The other one,' he said, 'got torn off my back by a woman desperate to have me.'

Coral smiled wearily. 'Of course.' It was a tired old joke. How odd, Bertie thought, that it should be true.

'Do I seem to you an absurd person?' he asked.

'No,' she said, 'not especially.' She snapped her case shut. It was a signal that she had little time for talk, and certainly none for what he had once overheard her call 'a therapy session with our Bert'. Deluded by her name, which still suggested to him a tropical paradise, Bertie had long ago, and very briefly, imagined he and Coral Strand might become lovers. Inwardly he now thought of her as the Head Girl.

'Not especially,' he repeated. It was hardly reassuring.

'About average,' she said, easing him into the corridor and closing her door. 'We're all a bit absurd sometimes, aren't we? See you tomorrow Bertie.'

He didn't go back to Marlow that night but spent it at his club. He has taken me there sometimes for lunch or dinner and I can report that it seemed a dreadful place where faded lackeys served tasteless food to dead men in suits. Bertie, however, finds some kind of ancient comfort in brown leather and panelled walls, and comfort was what he needed.

Next morning he went first, not to his office, but to the British Museum. After a lot of aimless wandering through the halls and galleries he found Arthur dozing on a chair in a corner among ancient clay burial urns. Bertie roused him with a sharp cough and said his piece: that he was very disturbed at what had happened. That it had not been as bad as it must have seemed (this in an attempt to allow for any story Shelley might have concocted) but that he wanted to apologise sincerely. That it had been his fault entirely, not Thelma's. That she should not be blamed – he took full responsibility. That it would never happen again.

Arthur didn't get up. He listened, staring with blood-shot eyes at a large broken urn. When the little speech was over he asked, 'You got fifty quid?'

Bertie was taken by surprise. For just a moment it seemed a wonderful relief, the possibility of doing something, paying something, by way of recompense, of absolution.

Yes, he said, he had fifty, certainly. He had more . . .

All the while scrabbling to get his wallet out, to get it open . . .

He held out a fistful of notes. There were at least fifty pounds, probably seventy. He didn't count, and there hadn't been a moment to reflect on what Arthur's request might signify.

Arthur beckoned him closer. Bertie leaned down over him, holding the money.

'Now stick it up your arse,' Arthur said, 'and fuck off outa here.'

Out in the street he seemed to have lost control of his legs. He ambled uncertainly in the direction of the City, still holding the fistful of notes, looking for a passing taxi showing a light and then, when one came along, not hailing it. He saw a florist's shop, went in and put the money down on the counter. What he wanted, he explained, was as many flowers as this would buy sent at once, this morning, to . . . And he gave her name and address.

'And for the card, Sir,' the florist said.

Ah yes, the card. He took it and after a moment wrote on it, 'To Shelley from Keats. Love you for ever.'

For the duration of the brief moment it took to write it, Bertie said, and for perhaps thirty seconds afterwards, he felt it was true.

I didn't quite believe – or was it just that I didn't want to believe? – that that was the end of the story.

'Just for thirty seconds?' I said. 'No more?'

He met my eye for a moment, shrugged, and looked down at the table between our comfortable chairs. 'Let's refill these glasses,' he said.

The Last Life of Clarry

❧

THE LORIKEETS ON THE RAIL WAKE ME. I'M AWARE OF them before I wake properly. They begin quietly as if they're making small talk and waiting patiently. I suppose they get noisier as they become hungry and quarrelsome, but it's hard not to believe they're slowly lifting the decibel level in order to get me up.

I roll out on to the carpet. That's a start. I'm grateful to the lorikeets. I don't like to sleep late, but when I'm alone . . .

And that hits me hard this morning. Consciousness – coming to it. Memory. She. They. I don't want to think about it. The purpose is what counts. Give it a capital. The Purpose. It consists of piles of typed sheets on the big table, scribbled all over with corrections and tidied on either side of the portable. Drafts. Re-drafts and revisions. Everyone used to tell me I ought to buy a word processor. Now no one tells me that, or anything. I see no one. I came here to be alone. I have the lorikeets.

I go to the balcony. They shift to left and right along the rail, making room for me. I think I can distinguish the boss pair – the couple who claim proprietary rights. The rest vary in number – anything from three to ten. This morning there are six altogether. Five. Seven.

Down there, eight floors down, is a school. The early

arrivers are there, running about in plastic raincoats, in and out of the shelter, with little bags on their backs. I don't want to think about them either. What is a passable way of saying that something 'tears at your heartstrings'?

Beyond the school are Simmons Point, Mort Bay, Ballast Point, Long Nose Point. Across the water a huge tanker has been tucked into Gore Cove. It seems to fill it. It must have been brought in during the night, or in the early hours of the morning.

I go through to the kitchen and do bread and honey for the lorikeets. They like brown sugar too, but Mrs Shrimpton, the old lady I met at the bus stop, told me if I filled them up every day on that stuff I might ruin their health. I thought at first it was only like giving them nectar. But watching them take it from the rail I noticed their short stubby tongues. They're not equipped for getting into flowers. I don't know about these things – I'm an amateur – but I want to treat them right. They're my companions – they and the magpies that come to the balcony at the front. The old lady said they needed seed as well as sugar, so I devised the bread and honey diet. They like it. They stand on one leg, hold the piece in one claw, and nibble at it. Sometimes one holds a piece while another nibbles. If you reach out to touch them they don't fly away in fright. They give you a hefty peck. Bugger off, I'm eating. No gratitude to the provider. But they will climb on to my open hand and eat off my palm. It's a nice feeling. And they're beautiful. Those extravagant colours – blue and green and orange and gold. On which drunken day of the Creation were they so splashed and daubed?

I came here to work. To work and to forget. To work is to forget – etc. Bullshit – but partly true. I'm writing a novel which is set partly in Auckland and partly in Los Angeles. For reasons which are not clear to me (and that may be a way of saying for no reason at all except the wish itself) I felt I had to write it in some place which was neither. Neither Los Angeles nor Auckland. So I came here. I live with these birds in the foreground, and long views (two directions) of Sydney Harbour and the Sydney skyline, while in my head I fight my daily battles, live and die and rise again, in Auckland and LA. They have become places of the mind. That's how it has to be.

Everyone is tired, I'm told, of the novel about the novelist writing the novel. Was it invented by the French Existentialists? I think I read somewhere that it was. (But what about Lawrence Sterne and the *Sentimental Journey*?) In any case, I'm not tired of it. I've written one and would write another if I thought it safe. Since it's not safe I'm defusing that impulse with these notes. The novel is about Auckland and Los Angeles. It is not about the writer in Sydney who is writing it. These pages are about him.

His name is Simon Dexter. He is forty years old. Forty-two. He has brown hair and good teeth except for one that was punched out in a game of rugby. In its place is a tooth on a bridge. He is the father of two, a boy and a girl. No more about that. The Purpose (it has to be said again) is all that matters. Everything else (and I mean everything – the world and all its wonders) is either irrelevant or it's material for fiction. There must be no third parties. No life but this one – the life that goes down on the page.

My breakfast is muesli and fruit followed by bacon on toast. And coffee. As I get older the start of the day gets more miraculous. It's as if I wake young again. It doesn't last, but there's that hour, or those few hours, when everything is jumping out of its skin. And because the brightness fades from the air, because it's not normal, it seems more marvellous than it did when one wasn't aware there was another, duller, more ordinary world underneath. And here I wake not only to the lorikeets and the bays I see looking west from my bedroom, but also to this view I have in front of me as I sit on a stool at the kitchen bench-table, spooning my muesli blindly because my eyes are taken up with this eastern down-harbour dazzle, the grand ugliness of the coathanger, the skyward mock-Manhattan off to the right of the picture, the ferries coming and going, the water-taxis, the orange-topped police launch, the black and white tugboats, the latest container ship in from Montevideo or Liverpool or the Gulf tying up across the water at Pyrmont. And just beyond the downward curve of the Bridge, one fin, two if I stand, of the Opera House.

I have the sliding glass doors open to the balcony at the front. From out there comes a whirl of wing and the strange pedestrian sound of my two magpies as they flat-foot up and down the rail or around the rim of the iron table. I take them cheese and some small pieces of meat. (Again I've been advised by Mrs Shrimpton.) They eat while I watch from an armchair, finishing my coffee and glancing (trying not to let my interest be roused by anything) at the front page of the morning paper. Unlike the lorikeets, the magpies are silent before they've been fed. It's only when they've finished that they do me a few cadenzas. It's my favourite bird-call. I close my eyes and see the green and brown river-flats of the Manawatu, which must have been where I first heard it; or the verandah of a hotel in a small northern New South Wales town. A fanning of feathers again and they're gone. I feel I've been thanked. Even rewarded.

This morning I've promised to call on Clarry. Clarry Shrimpton. He's the husband of the old lady I met at the bus stop. They live down near the ferry wharf in one of those typical terrace houses that have an upstairs verandah with an ornate iron railing. Like a lot of those houses, theirs has been spoiled by having the upstairs verandah built in. But it's unusual in that the railings remain, giving a strange baroque texture to the front face of the house.

I have mixed feelings about these visits. I'm not sure how I got myself committed to them, or why I haven't found an excuse to stop. I don't like them and yet I'm glad of them. Maybe in a way I do like them, but my expectation that I won't makes me feel as if they're an imposition. The fact is, Clarry is ill – very ill. There's been talk of chemotherapy. He says he won't have it – it makes your hair fall out. 'What hair?' she asks, and they change the subject.

Clarry has a single bed in the verandah room from which he can look out and down the street to the wharf. He keeps a watch by his bed – his wrist is too thin to wear it any more – and checks the ferries against a timetable. This morning he looks worse – thinner, his skin a strange brown colour – but he's sitting up, looking in good spirits. He has some money and some bets he wants me to place for him on the TAB.

They've had news their daughter in England is coming home. 'About time,' Clarry says. 'I dunno how she can stand them.'

'Them' is the Poms. Clarry hates Poms. But he hates Americans worse. He hasn't anything good to say about New Zealanders either ('present company excepted, of course'). They come over here and live on the dole. Bondi's full of them. Bludgers. New Zealanders are like West Australians, Tasmanians and Queenslanders – bloody hicks.

On my last visit, when Clarry was complaining about the Chinese taking over everything (he'd looked out and seen a Chinese bus driver down by the wharf), I asked whether there was any national group he admired. He said the Krauts had made bloody fine enemies. You could shoot a Kraut with respect.

Today he reminds me of the fireworks. He doesn't ask directly. He just says his daughter might be out in time to see them. I tell him again he's welcome to come and watch from my apartment. I don't see how it will be possible unless he improves – and I dread the thought of it – but I've said he can come, and I'll stick to that.

The first time I met Mrs Shrimpton (she hasn't invited me to call her Zoe) it was raining. I hadn't been long in Balmain and I'd always taken the ferry into town. But now a ferry had just left, it was wet, and I was wondering whether it might be quicker to take a bus. There was one standing down by the wharf. Its door was closed and the driver was sitting inside smoking. I tapped on the doors. He pressed a button and they opened. I asked whether this bus went into town. 'Ten minutes,' he said. 'Over there' – pointing to the other side of the street. And the doors whanged together, almost trapping me by the nose.

'They won't let you in until it's time.' That was Mrs Shrimpton. She was standing well back from the bus doors as if to signal she knew the rules. Rain was falling steadily. She had a bent black umbrella and she wore a raincoat. Also a piece of plastic tied over her hat, which was a kind of skewered beret in blue.

'It's terrible weather,' I said.

'Well it can happen in this country too,' she said. She'd picked I was a stranger. 'It has to rain, doesn't it. Where would we be without water? So long as you've got a roof over your head you've got nothing to complain about.'

I nodded.

'That's what I say,' she added.

I don't recall exactly how it was I allowed myself to be drawn into conversation with this person I might, in a more confident and happy state of mind, have dismissed as a piece of living history best forgotten. Somehow we got on to the subject of my bird visitors. She gave me advice about feeding them. From that (by now the bus had unclenched its doors and we were riding together into town) we moved to a discussion of the apartment I referred to as mine but which has really been lent to me by a couple who are travelling abroad. It was probably then the first hint was dropped about Clarry and the fireworks. She told me her husband had missed the tall ships. She explained it was the Bicentennial year (I knew) and that a re-enactment of the First Fleet had sailed into the harbour (I knew that too). But there were also the tall ships. They had come from all around the world as a tribute to Australia. Clarry Shrimpton had been too ill to walk up to one of the headlands or coves for a good look. She was hoping someone might offer a pozzy from which he could get a look at the fireworks that were scheduled for next month on the harbour. He'd read about it in the paper. He wanted to see the fireworks very much. Clarry Shrimpton loved fireworks.

It is indeed the Bicentennial year. You might think that's a good time to be in Sydney. For many people – especially Australians – no doubt it is. But for a writer trying to keep himself alive and well in two cities-of-the-mind called Auckland and Los Angeles, the Bicentennial is just a distraction. A nuisance. It's also (why not be honest?) a thundering bore. I've never known a country so bloated with self-regard.

The couple who own my apartment – old friends from long ago when I lived and worked in New South Wales – were here for the Australia Day celebrations and then left on their travels. They send me postcards. They like Singapore. It's clean, the shopping is wonderful. They're impressed by the Moscow Underground. They think it superior even to the Paris Metro. They find Dublin dirty (the Liffy, they tell me, is *brown*) but they love the Irish countryside and the western coast. But of course nothing matches dear old Sydney.

I become a misanthrope. The sheer effort of keeping my thoughts away from what I left behind (an average broken marriage) induces a kind of arthritis of the mind. Only there are those early hours of the day when I feel myself to be open and available to the world and so I'm able to work. After that the doors close. By evening there's only TV and alcohol to ward off despair.

What I find hardest to take is the school down there, eight floors down, as darkness closes in. Most of the mothers or fathers have come for their kids, but there are a few left with a distracted and irritable minder. The children play more frantically. I try to ignore them. Even from so far below I hear the voices coming up. I hear the minder shouting, 'Come down off that roof.' I go to the west balcony and look down. There they are, the last few, in their bright clothes, their bags on their backs, ready to go – running in and out of the lights shouting in that hectic way kids do when they're at the end of a long day, and anxious.

Today, while we were talking about the Bicentennial, Clarry said, 'Course, you know – I'm descended from a convict.'

'You talk a lot of rubbish,' Zoe Shrimpton said. She was bringing us tea and scones – she'd knocked up a batch, and there was jam as well. As she put down the tray she said to me in a loud whisper, 'It's the drugs.'

'What do you know about it,' he said.

'Come to that,' she said, 'we're all descended from the apes. According to Darwin.'

'Well, if you went up to Darwin you'd think so,' Clarry said. He let out a whinnying laugh.

After she'd gone he said, 'There's a lot she doesn't know. My grandmother saw the welts on his back. Thick as your finger.'

I've come up to the Cross for a change of scene. Auckland and Los Angeles haven't been treating me well. I remember the

Cross from my first time in Sydney, years ago. It seemed then like a first taste of Europe. I remember sitting out drinking coffee on the balcony of a hotel and feeling I was already there. Now I can't find that balcony or that hotel. I walk past the strip joints and the whores in miniskirts. I think seriously about going with one. They all look blotchy-faced or knocked about in some way – but that's not the problem. It isn't morality either, or conscience, or concern about the exploitation of women. It's fear. It used to be fear of VD. Now it's fear of AIDS. They say it's safe with a condom, but is it? And I'm not sure my machinery would work any more with one of those things.

It's Clarry who set me off on this train of thought. He has a way of craning his skinny neck to look around me, making sure his missus, as he calls her, isn't coming. Then he reaches under his bed, pulls out his money tin and his race books, and tells me what to put on for him at the TAB. Or if it's not racing, he comes out with some 'men's talk' that's not meant for her ears.

Today he asked how old I was. I told him thirty-nine.

'Thirty-nine eh. And who're you rooting?'

I told him I wasn't rooting anyone. 'I'm separated. Getting divorced, Clarry.' And I added, imitating his digger lingo, 'I'm on me lonesome.'

He nodded. 'So who're you rooting then?'

I felt like telling him he can be an irritating shit, but I think he knows that and he doesn't care. He has nothing to lose.

'You know how I know I've got it bad?' He pointed between his legs. 'Because the big fella won't stand up any more.'

'Give it time,' I said.

He closed his eyes and seemed to doze. I sat in the battered old basket chair by his bed hearing magpies somewhere out there. I closed my eyes too and saw green and brown riverflats. I might even have dozed for a moment. I was woken by Clarry's voice. 'It's like this,' he was saying. 'A man's programmed to root. All the rest's bullshit. You root, you're happy. You don't root, you're not.'

'What about love,' I said.

'Love's nice,' he said. 'But it's not necessary. Rooting's necessary.'

It made me think of a line of a poem by W.H. Auden: 'Thousands have lived without love, not one without water.'

I said, 'Some people would say it's the other way round.'

'Some people say all kinds of things,' Clarry said.

It wasn't that Clarry had provided me with a new philosophy, or a piece of essential wisdom. It has, really, more to do with what I'm calling the Purpose. I've come to think Clarry is dying and that I'm drawing the last life out of him and using it in my novel. It doesn't matter if that's codswallop. If it works, if it keeps me going, that's all that matters. But I've started to interpret what he says to me, as if he were some kind of oracle uttering obscure instructions from inside a deep cave. The cave is death. What is it telling me? That I can't create life unless I'm in some way immersed in it? What he calls rooting – I've hardly thought about it. Now he has made me conscious of it – conscious of a need.

So here I am at the Cross. It was a stupid idea to think I could pay some money and buy my way back into life again. But I sit out of doors under an umbrella near the Alemein fountain and drink what they call here a 'flat white'. I'm in a mood of gentle despair I know to be dangerous – like lying on a very comfortable bed for a moment when what you need to do is to get up and get going.

I take the long route to the TAB. I go down to Simmons Point and then along the foreshore into Mort Bay where the tugboats are tied up. Then up a street of ugly new townhouses and on up to Balmain shops. I don't go to the TAB to put Clarry's bets on. I go to find out the results, when I've missed the race commentary on the radio, and to get the odds. I don't put any of Clarry's money on the TAB. I keep it and pay TAB odds when he wins. I've become his secret bookie. He doesn't know. I don't know what he would think if he did.

It happened by accident. I forgot to put a bet on for him and the horse won. I thought it might distress him, so I pretended I'd placed the bet and I paid him the TAB odds. Then it occurred to me I could be a gambling man too just by betting against his bet. Some days he wins and I lose; other days I'm the winner. The amounts are never large. I think I'm ahead. I suppose the bookie usually is.

Today I came back from the TAB via the school. I stood outside the gates and looked into the yard. There's an open area with a broad sloping roof over it and benches underneath. There's one little girl who seems always to wear big baggy shorts and to have her hair held back from her face with a clip. She reminds me so much of my Emma at that age I suppose I always stare. Today I stood at the gate looking in. I ought to have known it would cause alarm. A woman came out and asked me what I wanted. I told her I was lost in thought. She didn't look reassured.

I came back here feeling as if I'd been beaten all over with sticks. But then straight away I sat down at the typewriter and I must have run through three pages with hardly a pause. It was the afternoon, when I don't usually write, and I finished those pages feeling I know exactly where I will take the story tomorrow.

So I cooked myself a meal, opened a bottle of wine, and felt it hadn't been a bad day. Now I'm sitting out on the balcony looking at the harbour by night. To say it's a beautiful sight is a ridiculous understatement. If it's true, as Zoe Shrimpton says, that there's to be a fireworks display on the harbour, this will be the place to be. But could Clarry be brought here? I don't see how.

I think again about his advice to me. Did he really say all that about 'rooting'? Or did I dream it in that dozy moment by his bed? I know it's normal enough to feel slightly deranged when you find yourself suddenly living alone after years of family life. The thought might bother me more if it weren't for the fact of those three pages written this afternoon.

Down on the water a paddle steamer is going past Pyrmont towards the Bridge. I take the binoculars from the living room and pick out the illuminated sign on its side: SYDNEY RIVERBOAT. Then I range over the city picking out the signs in lights – QANTAS, ESSO, ROYAL INSURANCE, HILTON, MARTINS, all in red; IBM, ARTHUR YOUNG, GOLD FIELD, in white; and CITIBANK in blue. On the North Shore ZURICH, MN and AGL are in blue; PHILLIPS is blue-green; SHARP and CIC are red; FP is white in a circle, and NCR white on red. LEGAL & GENERAL has a red and green umbrella over it. One of the tallest buildings overlooking the Quay has a sign of 1788–1988. Electric stars and spangles shower from it down the face of the building.

The phone rings. It's Caroline, calling from Auckland. It's late there – past midnight – and her speech is slurred. 'Have you been drinking?' I ask.

She wants to know what business that is of mine.

'You're in charge of my kids,' I remind her.

'Too right I am. And it's going to stay that way.'

'Is that what you rang to tell me?'

'Jesus, Simon, why are you such a bastard?'

'Why are you such a bitch?'

She hangs up on me. I phone her, but she doesn't answer.

It has rained for three days. The lorikeets come in the morning but after they've been fed they don't leave. They huddle, quarrelling, bedraggled, on the balcony rail. They move to the balcony below, or to the building next door, but for most of the morning they stay close. They're a distraction. I find myself getting up to give them more brown sugar or bread and honey. Then I recognise that I got up because I was stuck for a word or a phrase. It's only another version of straightening the pictures or making yourself a cup of coffee.

But the lorikeets don't stay all day. Late in the morning they begin to disappear. It's hard to imagine what mental processes prompt them into action. I watched one that had spent most of the morning on the rail. Suddenly it was in flight, out over Simmons Point towards Goat Island. It reached the island in just a few seconds but it didn't stop there. It flew straight on over and I lost sight of it, heading like a little green and gold rocket towards Waverton or Wollstonecraft.

As the rain clouds go over, bits of the city disappear. The Australia Tower and the tallest buildings come and go. Occasionally even the Bridge, straight in front of me there down the harbour, vanishes in cloud. But even when everything is clear and sharp, the rain goes on falling. It varies between heavy and very heavy. It never stops.

Today I went to a play at the Belvoir Street Theatre. I don't have a raincoat here, but I found a blue and white golf umbrella big enough to camp under. I took the bus into the Town Hall and set off on foot. I should have known that rain, like everything else in Australia, has to be on a grand scale. It poured through the shop verandahs wherever there was a weak point or a hole. It thundered on the umbrella, seeped through, and ran down the handle and up my sleeve. It turned the side streets into rivers. I kept looking out for a taxi but the few I saw had the engaged sign up. Going up Elizabeth Street, sheltering as far as possible under verandahs, I was soaked by a car steered by its happy-faced driver through the metre-wide flow of gutter water so everyone on the pavement was caught in the jet from its wheels.

The play was *Capricornia* from the novel by Xavier Herbert. The young hero grows up in Melbourne believing he's descended from a Japanese princess. When he returns, against advice, to Port Zodiac, he discovers he's what's known there as a 'yeller-feller' – half Aboriginal – and despised for it. That's the part of himself he has to learn to accept, and to make others accept. In the end he has to make a journey into the Outback to be reconnected with his tribe. He talks to an old Aboriginal woman. He tells her he hasn't any knowledge of the bush and how to survive there. She tells him not to worry. She gets lost in the bush too. 'Buy yourself a compass,' she says.

This morning when I went to my typewriter I was invaded by a terrible panic. I was sitting there thinking about those two cities-of-the-mind – the Auckland and Los Angeles of my novel – and I thought, 'Supposing no one believes in them.' It was like the brown sugar I put out on the balcony rail in the rain. My two cities lost their shape, sagged, sank down, spread out and were slowly washed away. In the end there was nothing but the wet black hard surface of the rail. I couldn't write a word. I didn't believe in them myself.

But I had nothing else to turn to. There were thirteen hundred miles of ocean between me and the wife who used to be 'my' wife, and the children who used to be 'my' children, and the house that used to be mine. This was not my apartment, my city, my country. I was here on the eighth floor of nowhere, and feeling so dislocated, so edgy, so precarious, it frightened me.

I couldn't write so I must walk. I trust in the action of walking, believe in its efficacy. It's something I can do, and here in Balmain all the water's edges, all the points and coves and bays which were once messy and jammed with nautical debris, are gradually being turned into parks and walkways. I walked around a big circuit of foreshore and finished back at Darling Street Wharf. It didn't seem enough and there was a ferry coming in so I took it and got off at Long Nose Point. I walked back along Louisa Street and through Balmain shops where I stopped for a flat white. It was there I remembered Clarry. I'd been neglecting him. I hadn't visited him since the rain began.

I found him much worse. You think a person like that can't lose any more weight – that there's no more to lose – but it isn't so. Today Clarry looked like a skeleton with skin. His head was a death's head. The dark pigmentation seemed to be spreading, as if he'd been baked over a fire. The wrinkles and folds were huge and dark. But the eyes weren't lifeless. The life still burned in them.

He couldn't reach down for his tin. I had to get it for him. The radio murmured from his bedside table while he fumbled and counted. Then he told me: there's a horse called Clan-ridden. He wanted me to put a hundred on its nose.

I hesitated. What would Zoe think? Wasn't a hundred a bit steep? I also thought about my own role as secret bookie. Did I want to bet whatever the odds were against his bet? I asked him was it an outsider. He told me not to worry my head about that. When I pressed him for an answer he said Clan-ridden wouldn't be a favourite but it ought to be. It was a dead cert.

I didn't know what to make of that, but I took his money.

He asked me about the fireworks. He said he'd been pretty crook since the rain started. Then he dropped off to sleep, his mouth open, a thin trickle of saliva running out at the corner. He snored faintly. He smelled bad.

I went out to the kitchen where Zoe Shrimpton was making tea. I asked her what was the date when the fireworks were to take place. She didn't say anything. She kept her back to me, clattering the tea caddy and the pot. It came to me that there were no fireworks. They might have been something she'd invented for Clarry to look forward to.

When I stuck my head around the door again he was awake. 'Clanridden,' he said. 'A hundred.'

'Clanridden,' I repeated. And I gave him the thumbs up.

When I got back here to the apartment I went straight to the typewriter. Auckland and Los Angeles swept back into my mind, dream-cities, fresh and clear and shining. I felt confident; and I felt I could see exactly how the novel is going to end.

I got up and stretched and walked out on to the balcony. The weather seemed to be clearing. Everything was clean except the harbour which had turned brown with the floodwaters that had sluiced down into it.

Then I remembered the race. I'd meant to go up to the TAB and put Clarry's bet on for him. I didn't want to play bookie if he was going to bet in hundreds, but it was too late now. There was only time to turn on the commentary. Clanridden won by a nose.

I owe Clarry $450. I think, 'I can't afford it.' Then I think, 'Of course you can.' Then I reflect on the 'I' and the 'you' in that exchange. And then I think, 'Four hundred and fifty bucks – it's a small price for the last life of Clarry.'

This morning the weather is clear, the sky blue, and there's a long brilliant track of glittering light stretching away down the harbour to the Bridge. The white faces of the terrace houses directly below look washed, and it's as if there are more trees among them, there seems (though it's an illusion) so much more green than when I last looked. The lorikeets bring their blue heads and gold-flecked breasts and green wings to the bedroom balcony but they don't stay longer than it takes to eat what I put out for them. On the front balcony the black of the magpies is blacker, the white whiter. And down on the water, three magpie tugboats are dragging that tanker away from Gore Cove and out towards the open sea. As it goes under the Bridge its highest point seems only a few feet below the centre span.

In the mail comes another card from my friends, owners of this apartment. They talk of returning. On the other hand spring has arrived in London parks and gardens, so they're not sure.

From home comes a copy of the *Listener*'s issue for the Bicentennial. It says New Zealand soldiers envied the vigour and style of their Australian cousins. Just a few days ago, on Anzac Saturday, the *Sydney Morning Herald* said the New Zealanders were the élite on Gallipoli because they combined the discipline of the British with the dash of the Aussies. How is it that we can be so civil to one another? It's so unusual it makes me uneasy.

Yesterday I met Clarry's daughter, Alice. She's very brisk and contralto, stylish, with faintly blue tinted spectacles and a young businesswoman's no-nonsense approach to traditional male pieties. She told me I wasn't to take any more bets for Clarry. That put me straight into my aggression mode. I told her I would do Clarry any favour he asked that it was in my power to do. She smiled as if to signal that her bullshit detector was in good working order and turned away. I had my instructions.

But Clarry didn't want to talk about racing. He held my hand and from time to time slipped into sleep, and maybe it was a coma. But in between there was something he wanted to say.

'I know where I'm going,' he said. 'No worries, boy.'

'Good on you, mate,' I said.

'Yeah, but . . .' He licked his lips. 'What about getting there?'

'What about it, Clarry?'

He frowned and screwed up his eyes. 'I might get lost.'

I wasn't sure how to respond to that. I just said the first thing that came into my head. 'Don't worry about it. Buy yourself a compass.'

His face was blank for a moment. Then the creases and wrinkles arranged themselves into something that could only be a grin. A kind of cackle ground its way out of his throat. Next moment he was unconscious again.

I put a roll of notes – $450 – into the tin under his bed.

The day Clarry died the lorikeets didn't come to the rail. Nature thought them too garish and warned them off. Or was it just that I slept late? The magpies came as usual, in their best black and white.

I'd finished the novel – or anyway a draft of it. Whatever kind of mess it was, it now had a beginning, a middle and an end.

Alice Shrimpton and I were getting on better, in the spirit of Anzac. She let me help with some of the arrangements for the funeral. Zoe sat helpless and desolate, as if she'd never allowed the thought of Clarry's death even a toe in the door.

And that night there were fireworks. I don't know what the occasion was – maybe the Queen's visit to open Expo 88. They seemed to come from somewhere beyond the Bridge and Bennelong Point, and they didn't last for much more than twenty minutes. But for that short time the whole harbour and the western sky were brilliant with eruptions and showers of fiery light.

I paced about with all the lights off – up and down the living room, in and out through the doors to the balcony. I was thinking of Caroline and the kids. More than once I began to dial home and then changed my mind and hung up. I set out and walked for almost an hour, around the foreshore and back along Darling Street. When I got back to my eighth floor and my double-locked door, the phone was ringing. I fumbled with keys, dropped them, put the wrong key in a lock and had trouble getting it out. By the time I got inside it was too late – the ringing had stopped. I dialled New Zealand.

'Were you calling me?' I asked.

'Calling you?'

'My phone was ringing – I thought it must be you.'

She was silent a moment. 'Does it ring so seldom?'

'No. Yes. Well – it doesn't ring all that often. I'd been thinking of ringing you. I suppose that's why I thought . . .'

'That was nice.'

'What was?'

'That you were – you know – thinking of . . .'

'Of ringing. Oh yes. I was.' Silence. 'So, anyway, it wasn't you.'

'No.'

'Well then. I'd better go.'

'What's the weather like over there?'

'It's been the wettest April since – I don't know. Since the First Fleet probably. What about Auckland?'

'We've had the driest since 1066.'

'Good on you.'

'What about the novel?'

'Finished. Well – a draft, anyway.'

'Finished! Congratulations. Is it good?'

'God knows. Probably not.'

'You must be feeling great.'

'I feel awful actually.'

The conversation ambled on like that for quite a long time. There was a kind of embarrassment about being so nice to one another. It would have been easy to slip back into terms of endearment.

∾

I don't usually weep at funerals. They have a strange effect on me. The closer the relative the more I go inside myself, hidden. Out there is a puppet, dry-eyed, going through the motions.

I didn't weep at Clarry's but I had to fight it. There was a lump in the throat and tears in the eyes. I don't record it with satisfaction. What was Clarry to me? The tears would have been for myself.

But sitting there in the unfamiliar church I had a thought. It was Clarry who sent me off on that wild goose chase to Kings Cross. But it was Zoe who gave me advice about how to feed the birds. There are more ways than one to skin a cat, and more than one to keep a man who's alone sane and in touch with the common life.

This morning I met Alice Shrimpton in a coffee bar just up from Circular Quay. It turns out she works for Amstrad, and she signed me up to buy a word processor. I've had to go into overdraft, but I think there's a royalty cheque due any day; and Alice is right when she says it will save me not just days but weeks of work now that I'm at the stage of slogging through my novel and making revisions.

The weather remains good though the nights are cool. I miss old Clarry. Zoe potters through her daily routines. She seems stunned. The lorikeets and magpies are here every morning. As I gaze out at it now, Sydney has begun to look, not ordinary exactly, but just like one more beautiful place. The world is full of them. I think of inviting Alice to come with me to my favourite Greek restaurant, but I'm still a little nervous of those faintly blue tinted spectacles.

Uncle Bjorn and the Saint of Light

RECENTLY I GOT THE NEWS THAT MY UNCLE BJORN Rosenstrom had died somewhere in the north of Sweden close to the Arctic Circle. That was not his own region – Stockholm was his city – but he loved the extremity of the seasons there, the weird white nights of midsummer when the sun never quite managed to set, the lovely blue-lit darkness of clear midwinter days when it never got itself above the horizon. According to the account of my cousin, he simply went for a long walk and didn't return. He was found two days later sitting under a fir tree, dead.

Uncle Bjorn was getting very close to eighty, so you might think he'd had his fair share of summers and winters. But he was evidently still fit enough to take long walks in the Arctic snows; and Swedes are folk who live into their nineties. I can't think of him as one who would take his own life, not unless something had been disclosed to him by his doctor – cancer, Alzheimer's disease, that kind of thing – in which case, of course, he would have taken himself off in precisely the tidy and efficient way a too-long walk in the frozen north would represent. But if there had been a medical reason for him to 'do a Captain Oates', I'm sure my cousin would have known about it.

Yet, on the other hand, Uncle Bjorn was a person so

efficient and rational, so much in charge of himself, and so knowledgeable about his country's northern territory and how to protect yourself there, it's hard to imagine him simply making a mistake. It's a puzzle which I have only been able to resolve by imagining him finding himself, in that almost-darkness of a clear midwinter day, in a state of exaltation, like Keats hearing the nightingale:

> *Now more than ever seems it rich to die,*
> *To cease upon the midnight with no pain*
> *While thou art pouring forth thy soul abroad*
>   *In such an ecstasy.*
> *Still wouldst thou sing, and I have ears in vain,*
> *To thy high requiem become a sod.*

I would like to think he died happy; and it's difficult for me to imagine otherwise. Uncle Bjorn was the most positive – the most terrifyingly positive – person I've ever known. In his head he was a good liberal; but in his body, in his behaviour, in his genes I suppose, he was an *ubermensch*. How could Death take him? How should His Royal Darkness dare to approach my blue-eyed relative, except tentatively, as a brother or a colleague, asking would he like to come now, or would he prefer a later date? I have to see it that way, some-thing subtly different from suicide – Uncle Bjorn discovering his moment, a kind of enlightenment that had brought him, not through pain or illness or grief or world-weariness, but mysteriously, by means of that blue northern half-light, right to Death's door among the fir trees. I imagine him in his long coat knocking there, like some ancient being in a fairy-tale, and saying, 'Okay, Darkness, I'm here and I'm ready. Now show me *your* region – and make it good!'

My cousin's letter included cuttings from Swedish news-papers about the death. Uncle Bjorn had been a well-known figure in Stockholm's theatre world – critic, expert on Strindberg, occasional director, author of one or two modestly successful plays, scriptwriter for movies and television. He was also famous for what had become known as the Summer Production. Every August he went to an island in the archipelago where he had bought an old farmhouse and barn and converted them for summer holidays. Over the years many artists and intellectuals had followed him there, buying up and converting farmhouses for holiday homes. Uncle Bjorn's barn had become their theatre, and each year they collaborated in writing and producing a play – the Summer Production. It was never published, never repeated, and no press or critics were permitted to see it. Consequently a certain mystique grew around it. Rumours would go about that this year it had been brilliantly written, wonderfully acted, incomparably staged, and so on. It was as if a whole Otherworld of the theatre existed, which only a few acolytes were permitted to visit and to experience.

This news of my uncle's death has sent me back to the notes I took when I first knew him. I was then on the brink of forty – a dangerous age for a man – and Uncle Bjorn was already into what ought to have been the safe haven of his sixties. My first visit was in late summer – he was just back from the island, very busy, and disappointed that I hadn't come in time to see the Summer Production. My second was winter of the same year, and I remember coming down over the airport between 12 and one of a clear December day, noticing the long shadows the fir trees cast, as if midday were late afternoon. This was partly a visit of my own, and a hotel room had been booked for me; but it was to be a family visit as well. Uncle Bjorn met me, delivered me to my hotel, and we agreed to meet the following afternoon when I was free and he would, he said, act as my winter tour guide.

Next day we met on the waterfront. It was not much past

the middle of the day, and there were even fitful breaks in the cloud-cover, but already the gilded façade of the Dramatiska Teatern was floodlit, and lights were coming on in shops and hotels. Through the glass front of the Royal Hotel that looks out on the harbour we could see the drifting figures of Nobel laureates and their entourages and accompanying journalists, assembling for the presentations that would be made in two days' time. Everywhere the windows that looked down on streets and squares were bright with red and green Christmas decorations and alight with pyramids of candles.

Uncle Bjorn was wearing a coat to his ankles and a broad-brimmed hat. There was a woman with him. I knew from my family that there was always a woman with Uncle Bjorn. It used to be that each new one was a new wife, but at some time in his forties he had given up marriage. Now they were just his women, each seeming more outrageously young and beautiful than the last. I heard my cousin once point this out to him, in a tone half of admiration, half of joking protest. But no, Bjorn replied, straight-faced but teasing; nothing had changed, except that he had moved with the times and given up the marriage ceremony. He had always, he pointed out, preferred beautiful women aged in their middle twenties. When he was in his twenties that had been his preference; it continued in his forties; and now, in his sixties, it was the same.

This new one, Ingeborg, was almost as tall as my uncle, and yes, of course she was beautiful. She had a large, pale face, almost a moon face, but the skin was delicate, without the faintest blemish, the brow and cheekbones high, the features finely chiselled, and the voice rich and musical and confident. She wore a long loose coat, which hung open, a long thin white scarf, and she carried her fur hat in her hand, so I was able to appreciate the thickness of her chestnut hair tied back loosely, but escaping in curls around her ears. I liked her so much and so instantly I felt a surge of jealous outrage that her hand should rest like that, lightly, possessively, and so at home, on my uncle's shoulder while he explained to me how we were to spend the day. Wouldn't it rest more appropriately (I suppose I was thinking) on mine?

They took me first to a museum where we looked at ancient runes on ancient stones, messages sometimes carved straight, sometimes in mirror writing, notifying the world of basic facts, like headlines in a newspaper: HARALD IS DEAD, with a simple line illustration of the hero on horseback, a shield on one arm, swinging a sword high over his bullet head with the other, and followed by two dogs. Out in a courtyard could be seen a huge Viking tent, a simple framework of ropes and branches covered with the furred skins of reindeer. Ranged along the galleries were Viking ships, Viking gold and ornaments, Viking armour, helmets, burial caskets and bones.

Uncle Bjorn explained to me how the Viking ships, with their terrifying beaked prows, could sail into the shallow waters of an inlet or estuary. A raiding party, he said, would be ashore in minutes. 'Anyone of any importance would be killed at once. After that, controlling the countryside was easy.'

We had a late lunch at the museum (of herrings, my notes tell me, with baked potatoes, beans and salad, and strong coffee) and then walked down to the waterfront where we took a ferry across to the old town. By now it was 3 pm, and quite dark. Climbing the cobbles, my uncle told stories about his time there as a student. In a square we stopped to listen to three blonde girls singing Christmas carols. An octave under them, Uncle Bjorn and I joined in, he in Swedish, I in English. Towards an hour that would have been evening in a New Zealand or an English winter, but which in Stockholm's December seemed already far into the night, Uncle Bjorn took us, Ingeborg and me, to a cocktail party at the apartment of his older brother, my Uncle Ivo Rosenstrom. Ivo had been a diplomat, working for the Swedish government sometimes in Washington or London or Paris, sometimes at the United Nations in Geneva or New York. He never married, and was always accompanied by a beautiful young man in his middle twenties. Like his brother, it seems, Ivo's tastes in sexual companion never changed, though the companions turned over even more frequently than Bjorn's.

The spacious rooms, candle-lit for the occasion ('Only once a year, dear boy,' Ivo assured me), with antique furniture and high moulded ceilings, were full of beautiful people, Stockholm's bourgeois intellectual élite. There was no alcohol – only tea and cake, the tea served in very large cups from a huge pot, the pot replenished constantly from a samovar. The cake was a kind of dry fruity Madeira, served with silver forks on heavy plates that matched the cups.

There was much talk about the Nobel Prizes. A beautiful woman was pointed out to me, a journalist who was, Ivo told me, the reason why a very famous European novelist had failed to get the prize. Long ago, after being assigned by her paper to interview the novelist, she had left her husband to become his mistress. The affair had lasted two or three years, after which she had moved on to someone else, a movie director; but the deserted husband, a member of the Swedish Academy, had thereafter, each year, spent his best energies lobbying effectively against the writer's nomination.

'There's an explanation for everything, you see,' Uncle Ivo said. 'Sweden believes itself to be a rational society and so we find a mystery intolerable.'

And yes, I could see that. There was something open and rational about Stockholm society – a special clarity. But it was clarity, not simplicity, and it could even seem at times mysterious, arcane, like those pyramids of candles in all the windows.

Light, lux, lucid – Lucy. That was where my mind took me, to the thought of the special attention Sweden gave to the saint of the December season, St Lucy, bringer of the new light, always represented as wearing it in the form of a crown of tall candles around her blonde head – but herself blind, her eyes having been torn out by dark tormentors.

That night as I crunched back along a street called Valhallagaten to my hotel, I felt excited and also faintly oppressed by the atmosphere of lurking strangeness, of dark threat, which this orderly community of high taxes and low road-toll, of the Volvo and the state liquor store, could engender.

Valhallagaten is very wide, with a tree-lined strip down the middle where the trams once ran – now a walking path, part gravel, part packed earth. Shallow depressions were filled with leaves and with ice that did not melt even during the day. I trudged along, my ears burning in the wind gusts, my hands sore with cold even inside the gloves of black leather I had bought in London for this visit. There was no one about. Sometimes a few flakes of snow or a small flurry of sleet would float down through the bare trees; but the air seemed too dry, the night too clear and cold, for a real snowfall. On either side, beyond the strips of roadway where cars sped by each with its perfectly sober driver, the tall, flat-fronted apartments replicated the pyramid pattern of the Christmas candles, as if all the interiors were uttering in unison the same word or phrase, singing the same few bars of the same song. To keep my spirits up I dredged up as many lines as I could recall of John Donne's poem, 'A Nocturnal Upon Saint Lucy's Day'. I managed the opening lines –

> 'Tis the year's midnight and it is the day's,
> Lucy's, who scarce seven hours herself unmasks.

Then I jumped forward to the second stanza where the poet declares his despair, matching, or even exceeding, the darkness of the season:

Study me then you who will lovers be
At the next world, that is at the next spring,
For I am every dead thing
In whom love wrought new alchemy.

With mutterings and whimperings of this sort I got myself to my hotel, the Arcadia, and went straight to the downstairs bar, which also served as breakfast room, where I knew the little Russian waitress would find me something to eat, and serve it with beer or wine. I liked this place with its ordinary food, its poker machine, and its decorated windows looking out on nothing but the peeling walls of dingy apartment blocks, so that one scarcely looked out at all, but enjoyed the interior life.

That night I dreamed that I was in a strange place with my sister and needing somewhere to sleep. I have two sisters, but the sister in the dream was neither of them. There was a single bedroom ready for her, with a neat bright bed and walls that seemed to be padded with soft cotton in colourful patterns; but I was led up into the roof of the building and told there was a stretcher-bed for me. It was very dark, and there was a loud metallic banging sound, as of boilermakers at work, or scaffolding being erected.

My sister objected. She insisted that I couldn't possibly sleep there – I must come down and share her room. Hers was a single bed, and we pulled the mattress on to the floor to give ourselves more space. We settled down together, but then, as if in sleep, we began to make love in the dark. I was enjoying it, but troubled. Then I remembered. 'You're my sister,' I said. 'We shouldn't be doing this.'

Next morning, in the little downstairs bar, as I piled my tray with a breakfast of coffee with rye bread and butter, tomato and cucumber, ham and a boiled egg, and thin slices of cheese, the dream came back to me. I tried to remember who this sister who was not my sister had been. It was someone familiar. I sat down at the window and closed my eyes, and at last it came to me. She was Uncle Bjorn's Ingeborg.

That evening we went to a dinner party at the apartment of a Swedish editor, Sverker Hansson. There were to be six of us around the table; but first we stood, drinking champagne and getting to know one another. Sverker Hansson came to fill our glasses and to introduce his daughter. Svenja was another tall blue-eyed blonde, like Ingeborg, the classic Scandinavian beauty. She was eager to talk to Bjorn about the Summer Production. She had heard so much about it, she said, and hoped one day she would find a way to see it, or better still to act in it.

Ingeborg had moved across the room and was standing to my left staring up at the bookshelves. I turned towards her and raised my glass. 'Skål,' she said, meeting my eyes as the convention requires.

'I dreamed about you last night,' I told her.

She smiled. 'That's flattering. Or perhaps it wasn't – I suppose it depends on the dream. I always feel flattered to think I should be . . . D'you know what I mean?'

'That you've been so far inside someone's head?'

'Yes. But I'm afraid I can't return the compliment.'

'Never mind,' I said. 'Some other time perhaps.'

'And was I nice?'

'You were very nice. Very kind. You were my sister.'

'Your sister.' She nodded thoughtfully. 'So what did I do?'

As I gave my mind to it, the dream came back, not just the facts of it, which were simple, but its atmosphere. I was aware it wasn't quite proper to tell a young woman you had dreamed of making love to her. I had stumbled thoughtlessly into this, and now I was stuck with it.

I said, 'Maybe I'd been thinking of Wagner.'

'Wagner?' She shook her head, not recognising what I meant.

'The brother and sister – Siegmund and Sieglinde.'

She nodded. 'Yes?'

'I mean,' I said, 'it was sexual, but not really physical.'

'Spiritual?'

'Yes, I suppose. I think it was . . .' And then I found the right word. 'Lyrical. It was like a poem – the dream equivalent of sex, but not sex.'

She laughed, and touched my hand lightly. 'Sex is never not-sex,' she said.

I had begun to tune in again to the conversation between the young actress, Svenja, and Uncle Bjorn who was becoming excited and raising his voice, bursting into short explosions of laughter. He was telling a story, partly in Swedish, partly in English, about how he had once kept a garden in which his best plants were eaten by . . . And here I was uncertain by what. Small animals of some kind – perhaps rabbits. Or was I misunderstanding? Was it that he needed to protect chickens from foxes? Whatever the exact nature of the problem, Uncle Bjorn had been told that in the long distant past, when the lion had roamed the European continent, these small animals which had become such a nuisance to him, had learned to detect and avoid ground where lions had defecated; and although the danger had long since passed for them, the genetic priming remained. Lion shit would protect his garden. The small marauders would starve sooner than approach it.

And then, on a visit somewhere far to the south of Stockholm – I think it was somewhere in Spain – he had met a zookeeper who said that for a small payment he would supply several plastic bagsful of the stuff.

So at the end of his holiday in the sun, Bjorn had set off on the long drive north with three bags of it in the boot of his car; and somewhere on that journey, skirting the edges of

Paris and going up into northern France, he had run into a police road-block. There had been an explosion in the Metro and they were searching for a terrorist. Uncle Bjorn had to try to explain to them what was in the plastic bags, and why he had it. Of course he hadn't been believed – they'd thought it might be a way of concealing Semtex. When at long last he'd proved his point, they were furious that this mad Swede, as they called him, had caused them to dig about in bags of evil-smelling lion shit.

It was a fine meal and a lively occasion. We all enjoyed ourselves; but especially, out-talking, out-shining us all, was my Uncle Bjorn. He told many good stories. It was not that he had lived a life that was in itself spectacular. He had been, as he put it, 'modestly adventurous' – no more than that. But strange things had befallen him, or things he was able in the telling to make interesting and amusing. We were all held captive to his high good humour, his literalness, his memory for fact, his eye for detail; and above all by what I had come to think of as his story-telling footwork, or perhaps it was the dramatist's sense of timing – the way he played things out in just the right order for the maximum effect. I had never seen him in such dangerous good form – a wise, handsome and wily owl, old yet ageless. And although his manners were perfect and he directed himself to the group at large, I couldn't help feeling that this display was especially for Svenja Hansson, the young actress who had made an effort to impress him and clearly hadn't failed.

Recently Uncle Bjorn had accompanied two writer-photographers on a part of their world tour which was to give them material for a book on the subject of death. One place they had visited was Benares on the Ganges, the holy city where those from the region whose families can afford the fifteen logs of wood it takes to burn a body, are cremated and their ashes scattered on the sacred river. He set the scene for us, the pyres spaced out at morning along the waterside; the noisy untidy groups of mourners each rushing a body, shoulder-high, through narrow streets down to the river; their happiness that their loved one is soon to move another rung up the ladder of creation; the small boats which take out into midstream the bodies of babies and small children which may not be burned; the holy men in their loincloths wailing prayers; and finally the river dolphins, the vultures and jackals, which clean up the remains and the unburned bodies – a whole ecology of disposal, a symbiosis between man and beasts, in which all is in balance except the ever-diminishing forests.

It was a description that left us all silent, wanting more; and so he moved on to Mexico, describing a village graveyard on the Night of the Dead, all the villagers gathered there, putting out, at first, sweet foods and drinks for the dead children, playing encouraging music, singing cheerful songs, to bring the little spirits out of their graves to be celebrated and honoured. Then came heavier food and drink for the adult dead – a kind of party which continued until morning, ending in drunkenness, riot and the sleep of utter exhaustion.

When Bjorn and I said goodnight in the street afterwards I was thinking we might not meet again for several years, unless I could persuade him to visit me in New Zealand. We hugged one another, he and I, I and Ingeborg. 'Thank you for dreaming of me,' she whispered, brushing my ear with her lips, and I walked away from them, under the bare trees of Valhallagaten between the apartment blocks with their banks of pyramid-candles, slightly drunk and feeling as if I were wrapped in a mood, an atmosphere, exactly matching the lyrical intensity of that dream.

But as it happened I was to see them only six months later. I was hardly home before a letter came inviting me to a conference in London late in July. So I was to be in Europe again, and in the summer. This was my chance to visit the archipelago, to see my Uncle Bjorn's house and barn on the island. I planned my trip with that in mind. I would be free to spend only a few days in Sweden; but I timed it so that I would at least see the preparations for the Summer Production, if not the finished performance.

The island was a beautiful tawny-green grassland of softly flowing lines always sloping towards the sea, nowhere heavily wooded, but with small areas of birchwood, and fir trees on headlands. Like most of the converted farmhouses, Uncle Bjorn's was of brown-painted weatherboard, with window frames done in dark red. The barn, which was very large – high and spacious and airy – was connected to the house, running off from it at right-angles. From all the upper rooms you looked down to the water and across it to the neighbouring island.

I was there only for a few days, and at the time when the Summer Production was nearing readiness for its final staging, so Uncle Bjorn was busy and preoccupied. He welcomed me warmly, yet I could see I was less present to him than I had been the previous winter. I wasn't bothered by this. It was as it should be. In fact it was reassuring to know that he wouldn't be deflected from his work by my visit.

But a change had taken place – the inevitable one. Ingeborg was gone, replaced by Svenja Hansson, who was taking a principal role in the new play. There was quite a group of people involved in it, but Uncle Bjorn and Svenja were at the centre, he controlling everything, she his instrument, totally pliant to his artistic will, and glad to be used.

It must have been the second day of my visit that I was climbing around in the barn-loft above the stage when a metallic clanging sound brought something into my mind, a feeling as of *déjà vu*, some place visited in the past, or some significant event. I saw there was a stretcher bed in the loft, and my dream of the previous Stockholm winter came back to me, the one in which I had made love to my 'sister'. This in turn made me recognise why the bedroom I had been given seemed so familiar. Though different, in its neat tight space, its small window frame, and the brightness of curtains and bedcover, it was like the one in the dream.

Next morning after breakfast Uncle Bjorn, frowning, took me aside. Ingeborg had phoned. She had come to the island and she would reach the house quite soon. This was a threat to his work, to his concentration.

'She's not supposed to be here,' he told me. 'She took the end of our affair very badly. They usually do, these young women. They think such things are forever. I want you to look after her. Persuade her there's nothing but pain for her here. She must go back to Stockholm.'

It was not a role I wanted, and I think I tried ineffectually to let him know I thought it was his mess, his problem, and that he should deal with it.

He looked surprised, and smiled at me in a way which suggested he thought me unsophisticated, not a man of the world. 'You don't approve,' he said. 'Well, never mind. I'm afraid this is how it has to be. Ingeborg is young, and the young are resilient. Someone has to be the loser in these affairs, and at my age, if I should wait until I were the one to be dropped, it would kill me. I wouldn't recover. You understand that, do you?'

Did I understand it? Not, I think, at the time; I was too much absorbed with what this new situation meant for me, whether it was, in fact, my opportunity, even perhaps one which my uncle was now contriving in order to get an unwelcome load off his own shoulders.

Ingeborg arrived late that morning. At lunch she greeted me like someone she only dimly remembered. I took her for a walk down to an inlet and she talked bitterly about her love for my uncle, and how badly he had treated her. I tried to give her (since in a way it was unarguable) the message he wanted her to hear and to accept: whatever the rights and wrongs of it, she could only hurt herself by hanging on. He was an old man. Why should she attach herself to his corpse?

She listened and didn't hear. She was absorbed in her pain, a mixture of jealousy and loss. Looking at her staring out to sea, tears in her eyes, a light breeze running its fingers through her lovely chestnut hair, I was impressed more than anything by the old man's power – that same power I had seen at work on the night of the Hanssons' dinner party. I told her I thought she should go back on the ferry next day. I said I would arrange it all and see her off. She didn't agree, but nor did she argue.

That night, late, when I was almost asleep, she came to my room. I was not surprised. So now, after all, the dream was to be fulfilled. She climbed into the narrow bed with me and began to talk again about her relations with Uncle Bjorn. My excitement, which had been extreme, slowly waned. I knew I must be patient, must hear her out, but the hours and the night dragged on, and still she talked about her love for this old man, sometimes weeping, sometimes laughing with pleasure at a happy recollection. I felt myself expunged. I was not there. I was only a physical presence in the half-dark, someone to talk to – anyone would have done. I was very tired, and sometimes slept for a few minutes and woke to find her still talking, not having noticed that my attention was less than perfect.

The curtains were apart and the twilight went on and on. At last, somewhere in the brief time between the extinction of the light and the birds' first excited announcement of sunrise, we made love. For her, I knew, it was no more than a way of saying 'Thank you', a small gratuity for my patience and my attention.

Next day, as I got her to the ferry, she was more cheerful and affectionate. She apologised for having 'unloaded all that' on me. I wasn't even sure she remembered what we had done in the hour of darkness. 'Tell the old bastard I'll come to his funeral,' she said. 'But I'm sure he knows that.'

As the ferry sailed out she waved from the rail, and smiled, and shook the hair back from her face. Her crisis was over. I never saw her again. I retain the fact of our having made love as something known rather than as a memory; the dream, on the other hand, is as vivid as if it belonged to the night before last.

But setting down these recollections has made me think again about my uncle's death. In particular I've thought about that exchange between us on the island when he noticed that I was in a mood to reproach him for his treatment of Ingeborg, and he shrugged it off, saying that since one of them had to suffer it was better it should be the one who possessed the resilience of youth. I've thought, too, about the fact that my cousin said there was no one with Uncle Bjorn on his final visit to the north. I've imagined him making that long train journey alone, staring out into the darkness, watching the blue light of the sunless day come and go over the fir forests and the leafless birchwoods. When had Bjorn Rosenstrom ever been alone before? It was unheard of. Had he at last, a man closing fast on eighty, found himself in the role of the one deserted, lacking the strength to rise above his sense of loss?

But it was not in my Viking uncle's nature to run away; he went always *towards*. And now I've remembered the ending of that poem by Donne, 'A Nocturnal Upon Saint Lucy's Day':

> *But I am none, nor will my sun renew.*
> *You lovers for whose sake the lesser sun*
> *At this time to the Goat is run*
> *To fetch new lust and give it you –*
> *Enjoy your summer all.*
> *Since she enjoys her long night's festival,*

Let me prepare towards her, and let me call
This hour her vigil and her eve, since this
Both the year's and the day's deep midnight is.

At last, and for the first time, he must have felt he was truly alone, and that he no longer had the strength it would take to begin again. The summer would not again deliver him the 'new lust' it would bring to younger lovers. So he travelled north (or so I mythologise him) into that blue sunless light of an Arctic midwinter, and walked out through the deep snow-drifts for his final assignation, not this time with any human lover, but with Saint Lucy, the blind blonde with candles in her hair.

Of Angels and Oystercatchers

ONDAY: (BLOODY MONDAY). REPLY FROM REGISTRAR, ie Promotions Advisory Committee, ie HOD (blame him? Not altogether. But, yes) to say application for Promotion to Associate Professor declined – this in the week of turning fifty, turning the corner, going over the hill – the landscape of eternal Senior Lecturerhood ('Specialist in Commonwealth Modernisms') stretching away. Fate, you desert flower, you mercenary, you crippled smith, you fucking fairy – you are not kind. Does the Applicant's present (and pioneering) work on the poetry of Alban Ashtree count for nothing? Or was it considered by those magisterial unworthies, sheersmen, ball-breakers, punks-on-high, that Ashtree's being Canadian rendered him less significant than . . . etc etc Shakespeare, yes. Wordsworth, certainly. T. S. Eliot, why not? Witi Ihimaera, okay. But Alban Ashtree? Never heard of him!

Well, you dark darlings in your committee-corner: that is something that may change; and it may be 'the Applicant' who will bring it about. At least he doesn't propose to give up on Ashtree. Not yet.

He? Notice, please (as he has himself just noticed) that in this journal only now taken up, not touched since his leave as 'Distinguished Visitor' to Quinton campus, Alberta, Canada, interrupted it, the discourse is past its second, and now well into its third, paragraph – and still no first person pronoun. This has not been policy; not decision. Does it tell something about its author, his state of mind?

'His'? Let him be 'He', then (and let there be light!). Is such possible? A diary in the third person? 'He did this, he did that . . .' 'He' short for Henry. 'Henry' long for the ninth letter of the alphabet. Henry Long? No. Henry Bulov, otherwise (or once) known as 'the Fly', and reminded of it, as recently as this morning, by Kevin on the balcony. Kevin-in-his-socks O'Higgins – drainer, leftist, old schoolmate: 'What's all this Bulov bullshit, Henry? You were Blow then; you're Blow now.' No use telling him that Bulov was the family name; that grandfather changed it during the '14-'18 War, when anti-German sentiment ran rife; that Henry went back to it long – thirty long – years ago. Kevin knows. The change unsettled him then, and still does. He wants his past undisturbed, and if Henry Blow is part of that past Henry Blow should not be erased by a stroke of the pen. Or is it just that Kevin likes to think of his old mate as the Fly? 'How many miles to Babylon? Three score miles and ten' – and Kev liked to add, '*as the Blow flies*!'

3 July: They, Kevin and 'he' – third-person-Henry – looked at old drainage maps this morning. Karaka Crescent: once Violet Crescent. There must have been a small stream down here, dry in summer, flash-flooding in winter. Now drains run in what was the stream bed. Kevin's team is putting in new pipes, separating sewage and stormwater; having problems because the fill is soft, trench sides collapsing, buried logs (big ones) blocking the digger, chainsaws grinding and groaning and stalling eight feet below lawn-level. Days of work lost. Kevin grumbles.

Working at home a couple of mornings each week, Henry talks to Kevin when he stops for coffee. Invites him, bootless, up on the balcony. Even Kev's socks shed mud-flakes. Their talk is what K calls 'ketchup'. Henry explains: 'Alban Ashtree was a Canadian poet killed in an avalanche in the Austrian Alps. I study his work – will write about it.' Kevin explains: 'I left the Party years back – have a new wife.' More than that – much more; but that is what it comes down to.

Kev's first wife was the hard-and-fast Marxist, though he used to deny (still does) that she talked him into it. Says his Marxism came from the heart. 'What would you expect? Dad a wharfie locked out in '51; mum first woman vice-president of the Labour . . .' (Something-or-Other. Henry, author of these notes, can't afterwards remember) '. . . Council. That was in the days when Labour meant "the socialisation of the means of production, distribution and exchange".'

Kevin left university to 'join the workers'. 'Undergrad' became 'Undegreed', as he wrote to Henry a few months later, and then 'dungareed'. Worked as a drainlayer. Became a contractor; bought equipment, diggers; 'graduated' to heavy machinery, got rich, went broke, learned to lay off workers, got rich again . . . Now he looks around his old mate's modest house, full of books, paintings, the academic detritus of decades. Always nods thoughtfully, appreciatively. 'It's nice.' You could see it this morning – he wouldn't mind living like this rather than in the steel and glass palace up on the Remuera ridge he bought with Wife-2, Cheryl. She's a modern young business woman, something to do with the stock exchange (Futures Market?) with big padded shoulders and a briefcase.

'I'm still a Marxist,' (this was Kev on the balcony); '*in theory*, mate. It's just that in the real world theory's got no battalions. No bullets. No *balls*. You with me?'

And yes, Henry was 'with him', if the question meant did he understand. 'In *practice*,' Kev goes on, 'I just hate fucking unions, mate. I've had to deal with them. And Welfare State bludgers; and Maori whingers; and especially I hate white liberal wankers.'

4 July: Lay in bed this morning ('he' did) wondering is he still a 'white liberal wanker', and if he is, how is it that he doesn't dislike Kev? No. More than that – *likes* him; likes him best when he says those unacceptable things . . .

Remembering school and Kevin. Chess. Crossword puzzles – more and more difficult ones, filled with anagrams. And swapping books – Edwin S. Ellis, James Fenimore Cooper, Rider Haggard, Robert Louis Stevenson, Charles Kingsley, John Buchan, Baroness Orczy, Conan Doyle – *stories* (fuckit!) – was reading ever so good again? And the experiments they did together in mental telepathy: communicating colours and numbers with a success rate far beyond statistical probability . . .

Thinking about overhearing Kevin's team ribbing him in the trench about 'a hard day's night' with Cheryl, twenty years younger. Remarks about 'shagger's back' and being 'saddle sore'. And then Kevin telling him up on the balcony, away from the lads, that his new sex life is 'very nice and relatively quiet. Cosy.'

Strange to have old mate Kevin and his team digging up the front lawn!

Paste xerox from *Mountain Safety Manual* here:

> Avalanche rescue: In most avalanche accidents rescue of trapped victim(s) depends on the action of the survivors. Organised rescue from afar usually turns into a body recovery. Fifty per cent of avalanche victims suffocate if not uncovered within 30 minutes. Survivors must not panic, but must note with respect to fixed objects – trees or rocks – first, the point on the slope where the victim was caught, and second, the point where last seen.
>
> Sliding snow flows like water, faster on the surface and in the centre than on the bottom and at the sides. When an avalanche follows a twisting channel the snow and the victim conform to the turns.

After an escape route has been chosen and lookouts posted to watch for further slides, the rescue party hurries down the victim's path, scuffing their feet through the snow to uncover clues – items of gear, or his avalanche cord. They look around trees or outcroppings which might have stopped him, and beneath blocks of snow on the surface. They shout at intervals, then maintain absolute silence while listening for a muffled answer.

Henry listens to the silence. The white slope glistens in the winter sun. Ice drips from the fir trees. The echo of the survivors' call goes down the mountain slope and across the valley, and comes back from the other side. There is no 'muffled answer' out of the beautiful treacherous snow. Thirty minutes, and then suffocation. The last of the poetry is squeezed out of Alban Ashtree.

Friday (evening): This morning over coffee, Henry talked to Kevin about Alban Ashtree. And about crosswords. They had a shot, as in the old days, at making anagrams. Tried 'avalanche'. The drainlayer came up with 'a leach van'. Did it in his head. The Senior Lecturer (for life), who always suspected Kevin was smarter, used a pencil and took longer, but produced 'have a clan'.

As in, for example, 'Four down (9): Have a clan in the Highlands? Be careful.'

The advantage of this clue (they agreed) is that the experienced crossword solver, alert for an anagram, won't know whether 'have a clan', 'highlands', or 'be careful' contains the nine letters in which the wanted word is concealed.

Same coffee break/smoko Kev pointed out that Alban is an anagram for banal. Henry replied that Kevin is an analogue for cunt. Kev thumped him one on the upper arm. They were back in the lower sixth.

Sat: Ashtree's last poem sequence looks very 'Post Modern' – double-margin (ie some lines justified left, some right); lack of ordinary punctuation; fractured grammar and syntax; sense of a voice speaking straight out of the text. Yes. But when all that's set aside, what is offered the reader? Stories. Anecdotes. Can too much be made of the narrative element? Maybe; but much more likely to make too little, it so easily passes unnoticed. (In lit as in life, everything becomes Story.)

Henry mentioned this to Kevin yesterday. Kevin said, 'The Big Bang theory never made sense to me. Why should everything start from nothing?'

End of conversation. Now, writing it down, Henry wants to give 'everything' and 'nothing' capital letters. 'Why should Everything start from Nothing?' And (he asks himself) how is it that drainlayer Kevin's remarks often seem not quite intelligible, but pertinent? He was always like that.

8 July: Henry's call at HOD's office. HOD had just been notified that Henry didn't get promotion. Wanted to say that he had supported Henry 'to the hilt'. 'Et tu Brutus!' – that sort of 'to the hilt'? was what Henry wondered, and it may be supposed HOD saw Distrust Writ Large on these paranoid features because he said no more – went to his filing cabinet and pulled out the confidential memo he'd sent to the Promotions Advisory Committee. Double embarrassment for Henry: because HOD had said such nice things, especially about the work on Alban Ashtree. He has been on the phone this morning to find out what went wrong. Thinks Henry's case was spoiled by the English Department's own rep on the Committee, the little Punk theorist whose name eludes Henry. He (the Punk) is reported to have told them that Henry Bulov said 'Fuck theory' in a department meeting. This turned the woman from Sociology against. And then the Maori rep, who had been *for*, because he thought Ashtree was a Native

American, changed his vote when the Punk told him it wasn't so – Ashtree was purest Anglo. That turned it around.

All hearsay, HOD points out; nothing of these meetings is supposed to be reported, so there's nothing to be done. But for the record (what record?) Henry Bulov did not say 'Fuck theory' in a department meeting (though he thinks it often enough). All he did was to report, by way of an amusing anecdote, the graffiti he saw on the Quinton campus: 'Theoreticians are Saussure they know everything, but they know Foucault about anything.'

But there's worse. (Should this be written down?) Last week when Henry told Kev about his non-promotion and grumbled about HOD, Kev said in such situations it was always best to hit back – hard: 'Better to harry than to burn. You sleep better.' So Kev went to the phone and called a company that delivers chicken shit by the load. Gave HOD's name and address. Ordered some vast amount, explaining that he and his neighbours had a 'co-operative gardening venture' and would share it around. 'Just tip it on the drive, mate. We'll barrow it away, no sweat.' It's to be delivered today. Henry can't phone and cancel – doesn't even know the name of the company. It will be there in the drive awaiting HOD's homecoming.

Late-at-night (when dark postscripts make best sense): Note that among personal belongings of Alban Ashtree found in his Quinton office after news of his death came through from Austria was a small squarish automatic pistol and some rounds of snub-nosed ammunition – a luggage label tied to it, the name Alban Ashtree and address printed on one side; on the other, DRINK ME. It's idle to speculate, but . . .

Chewsday. Film Society: (Anne likes to forget the law, Henry to forget literature.) This week it was *Wings of Desire* by Wim

Wenders – about two angels whose beat (wingbeat) is Berlin. They're benign but their world is black and white. At first you only see it as they see it. Then there are brief moments when you see the human world – in colour, which both angels crave. One opts out of angelhood and joins the human race. Now it's all colour, with only flashbacks to the drabness of the angel experience. The ex-angel is obsessed with a beautiful trapeze artist (cf Picasso?). When they meet and fall in love she makes a speech about a new world, which sounds like the old one, with colour and biology, men and women, love and sex and rock music and cities and vividness and action – except that now it's to be angel-less.

The war (the big one) belongs in black and white – like old newsreels. The burning cities, the dead laid out in rows among the rubble, the living searching among them for familiar faces, the piles of fallen bricks and smashed concrete, the swastikas, the Jews herded into gas chambers – how is it that Wenders sees all that as the world of angelicism? Because (Henry thinks) it came of a belief in solutions – *final* solutions. The angelic order and the theoretical abstract were Nazism's close cousins. Germany went the whole way – burned right through to rationality's non-human end. It did the unspeakable and learned there was no escape from death, only a vacation from it, taken in hell. The price of life's full colour range is acceptance that it is subject to limit. (The temporal is temporary.) Also that eternity is only the Other by which time defines itself.

Henry walked out into the night wondering what it would be like to feel there really was a new world beginning; that the angels had had their day; that people would learn to live in their bodies, which meant in their minds too, but minds as parts of bodies, not minds as winged instruments of escape, space vehicles, chariots of vain hope.

11.7: Another xerox from the *MSM:*

> When something has gone wrong swift action may be less
> effective than correct action. On the mountains, once any
> person is beyond voice range, the party has lost control over
> his subsequent actions. So there must be no hasty separation.
> Everything must be planned, prearranged, including what
> every member is to do under every conceivable circum-
> stance, until he has completed his part in the rescue.

'Aren't there any women in them there hills?' That was Rachel
calling by (she wants to borrow some books and do her
washing) and reading over Henry's shoulder. He told her
there is, or there was, something called (he thought he
remembered from an age-gone-by) the generic pronoun
which is, or was, genderless – as in 'He who hesitates is lost.'

Rach said, 'Thanks for that, he,' ruffling old Father Time's
grizzling hair.

Since when he has been sitting here imagining Ashtree
looking up, pausing to watch the avalanche snow sweep and
swerve and flow down the mountain slope; then, too late,
making a run for the side of the gully. 'He who hesitates . . .' Or
did Ashtree stand there saying, 'Come and get me!'? Was he
suicidal? Is that how the last poems, the ones about the
Snow Maiden, should be read? – that his Muse was Death? Why
else the pistol? – and the tag with DRINK ME printed on it?

Also this morning came a letter from friend John E.,
experienced mountaineer (he once nearly died dangling at the
end of a rope in a crevasse on Mt McKinley in Alaska) now
living in Seattle. John says he has heard nothing of the
accident in which Ashtree died. Asks was Ashtree with a party
or (would he have been so foolish?) climbing solo? John will
ask climbing friends to check on it. He goes on, 'The mountains in Austria are lovely, on a New Zealand scale. Avalanches
certainly happen there, usually in winter and spring. Warnings

go out, but people still get caught. This last spring we were on Monte Rosa (Switzerland) from the Italian side. Climbed the second highest peak in Europe by a spectacular route with an Italian guide, our communication being pretty much restricted to musical terms – presto, lento, bravo, etc.'

At the bottom of the letter he has done a black and white sketch (is he an angel?) of a mountain landscape with dark rock-faces, white snow slopes, and fir trees.

Later: The thought has just come again to Henry, like a rush of blood, about the refusal of promotion – the injustice that a committee of mind-mongers, theory-thugs, PC-pushers, *Angels*! – should have . . . etc etc.

Why does he stay? He's only (that was brave!) fifty. The world's big, the opportunities are still there. Anne's legal talents are equally exportable. The children are on their feet and self-sufficient. On their last sabbatical in London some-one asked Henry why he was going back to New Zealand. He replied (without thinking, but now considers it at least a dignified answer), 'I don't live to be entertained.'

Thurs 12th: Last night's video: *One Flew over the Cuckoo's Nest*. The world is a lunatic asylum. Every bureaucracy, every human institution, is a lunatic asylum. (New Zealand in particular is a lunatic asylum – but that's Henry's inter-polation.) McMurphy (Jack Nicholson) is there in the bin because he has too much life for what's conceived to be the common good. Like an over-spiced soup he must be diluted. Those experts who sit around a table deciding his fate are his Promotions Advisory Committee. McMurphy, they say, 'may not be psychotic; but he's *dangerous*.'

McMurphy's breaking of the rules is pure energy, 'eternal delight'. He bounces back from shock therapy with all his old chutzpah; but that only ensures worse is in store for him. His violence, when it comes, is *protest* – moral indignation. Oh Henry, you have been there! Even if only as metaphor, those desperate calm corridors are known to you. You have spent half a century looking into the cold eyes of Nurse Ratchet, your country's tutelary goddess. How is it that you don't carry the final scar, the spiritual lobotomy? Or (frightening thought) has it happened and you don't even know?

(Evening): Anne is preparing for depositions in her murder case. She has brought home documents and a book of forensic photographs (in colour!). Henry takes a few quick looks and winces away. She has become (almost, she says) used to them. He reads the three separate statements made by the accused. In the first he says a strange man wearing a feather earring did the killing. In the second he says he did it himself; says, 'I was growling like an animal.' In the third he says it was done by the wife of the deceased. The Crown case is that the wife persuaded him to do it, rewarding him in bed, before and after. The accused is a Maori aged 17. Anne intends to argue for the defence that the second statement should be set aside because at the time he made it he was asking to have his mother with him and the police refused.

Now Henry has just had a longer look at the photographs. The dead man is Polynesian, but in death the brown skin has faded to a sickly grey. He has huge wounds which have been stitched because he didn't die at once. The stitching looks rough, as if done by a maker of fishing nets.

What Henry felt was disgust. He and Anne have just had an exchange which went roughly as follows:

H: The second statement's the incriminating one.

A: It is.

H: So if you get that struck out, there's not much of a case left.

A: Not much. No.

H: And you think because he was asking for his Mum . . .

A: He's only seventeen, Henry.

H: D'you think he did it?

A: That's irrelevant, darling. This is a point of law.

H: Oh sorry. I was thinking about all those knife wounds. Silly me.

A: Well, of course he *did* it . . .

H: Ah!

A: Henry, I say, 'Of course he did it.' But that might be wrong. That's why it has to be 'due process'.

H: You mean 'due process' is never wrong?

A: No. It might sometimes produce a wrong result. But when it does, no one's to blame.

Friday the 13th (sowatchit!) and Kev came to the door early. The digger had broken into an old clay pipe. Kev thought it must be the existing sewer, but it wasn't where it ought to be. Henry was able to put his mind at rest. The pipe they'd broken into was an even older one, not used any more except unofficially for taking field-tile drainage from lawns and gardens.

Must put down Henry's dream before it's forgotten:

They (he and Anne) were in London, the two of them walking through streets that got narrower, more ruined, filled with debris, fallen beams, dust, wreckage. He was vaguely worried, trying to remember where they'd left the children. They came to a dinner table and sat down. It was properly laid – cutlery, candles, flowers, wine, glasses, napkins. Well-dressed people sat around making polite and witty conversation; but all about them lay the ruins of the city. Henry began to talk to them about his research. It had to do with Austrian milk-vendors.

HOD makes no mention of chicken shit. Was it delivered? Did it go to the wrong address? Henry can't ask, and if HOD doesn't choose to speak of it, he will never know.

Bastille Day: 'Allons enfants . . .' Henry sings, celebrating two hundred years of froggy bullshit. Remember (he writes in his diary!) the story about the Chinese Communist Government official on a visit to Paris asked what, from a Chinese point of view, had been the significance of the French Revolution in world history. Chinese official replied, 'It is too soon to say.'

Kev's team is now two doors down the street. Watching them, Henry understands something about unemployment. They dig down more than two metres, a trench wide enough for two pipes (a big and a bigger) side by side. By hand, that would take how many men how long? The digger does it in no time. When it comes to a hedge it lifts a section out, roots and all, to be put back later. The trench runs dead-straight across the fronts of four properties. Back at the last set of man-holes two laser beams are set to fire a pencil-thin beam of red light straight through the centre of each pipe. As long as the beams make bullseye hits on targets set in the far ends of the pipes, the drains are laid dead straight and there's no need for a surveyor to check.

The team works in pairs. Kevin and his mate dig out the trench, put in the pipes, and fill as they go. The second team comes up behind, laying topsoil over the disturbed clay, replanting grass, replacing concrete paths, hedges and gardens. The second team also does the new drainage around the houses, separating sewage and stormwater and bringing them down to the new lines. This part of it has to be done by hand. But the narrow-gauge pipes around the houses are plastic now, where they used to be clay.

Sunday: Here's a true story: Last evening Henry and Anne went to a little Italian restaurant in K. Road, the Quattro Fontane. Just half a dozen tables, one waitress, and the owner, Frederico – first-rate cook, amiable host, loud, flamboyant, banging his pans around, shouting jokes and orders over his shoulder, singing, sending flames up to the ceiling.

Henry had his back to the kitchen. Anne watched Frederico and worried. He should go more slowly. No need for all that drama. One day he'll blow up etc.

No more than ten customers all evening; and late, when most have gone, Anne sees Frederico go behind a curtain to a little room – or space – under the stairs. Now she has tight hold of Henry's wrist. Something's wrong. Frederico is having some kind of seizure – she can see the curtain moving violently. There's a thump as he hits the floor, a groan just audible over the Pavarotti tape. She's sure he's having a heart attack. Henry must go and help him.

Well! It can be said, it will be imagined, that Henry was not keen. He'd had a lot of red wine. He didn't want to know about heart attacks. There was a predictable exchange – How could she be sure that . . . ? How could he ignore the needs of . . . ?

So now Henry gets up and lumbers towards the curtain behind which, despite Pavarotti's best efforts to drown it out, there is indeed occurring some kind of heaving and groaning. Henry pulls the curtain back. Frederico is down on the floor, right enough. Face down. But the waitress is underneath him. There is a general impression of clothes pulled up, pulled down, got out of the way without being shed. Frederico is riding up and down on a gentle swell. The waitress is smiling. Her eyes drift over an ocean of content, then heavenward over Frederico's shoulder where they meet . . . Henry's! They widen, scrunch up into a frown. She begins to beat the cook's shoulders with her small fists, hissing at him, 'Get off me. Leave me alone.'

Henry lets the curtain drop and returns to his table. He tells Anne Frederico is okay. He's just lying down – so to speak.

Anne wants to know what 'So to speak' means. He tells her. She nods. They stare at one another, hands over mouths, trying not to laugh. She apologises.

Henry shrugs and says he supposes it's one kind of heart attack.

16 July: Henry has been thinking again about Wim Wenders and his angels in *Wings of Desire*. He writes into his diary two lines from a poem by Edgar Allen Poe which Janet Frame (who has an angel at her table) quotes in one of her novels:

> The angels not half so happy in heaven
> Went envying her and me.

This quotation sends him hunting for an essay about Poe by Allen Tate, 'The Angelic Imagination'. He finds it and copies sentences:

> The human intellect cannot reach God as essence; only God as analogy. Analogy to what? Plainly analogy to the natural world; for there is nothing in the intellect that has not previously reached it through the senses . . . Since Poe refuses to see nature, he is doomed to see nothing. He has overleaped and cheated the condition of man . . . Man as angel becomes a demon who cannot initiate the first motion of love, and we can feel only compassion for his suffering, for it is potentially ours.

31 July: Another month gone. So has Kev with all his machines and men and reminders of the long-ago. Work on Alban Ashtree is suspended – maybe for ever. Bob Wilcox has written from Quinton explaining why Henry has had no formal replies to his enquiries. There is, it seems, some uncertainty about where and how the accident occurred which killed Ashtree. It is supposed to have happened in Austria, but the only accident of that kind at that time occurred in Switzerland. Meanwhile the Canada Council has said the substantial amount it has put up for posthumous editing of his works is available only to Canadian scholars; but the funds are frozen until a death certificate has been received.

Henry thinks it a nice little irony (anger management teaches him to avert his eyes from the larger one) that Canadian funds have been 'frozen'. But Switzerland? He is sure Ashtree would have wanted death by alliteration: killed by an avalanche in the Austrian Alps.

Summer (Whangamata): Henry has been glancing through this notebook which he has neglected for – how many? – months. Its contents have faded along with the memory of Quinton and his excitement at the idea of being first to publish a full-length study of Ashtree's poetry. This morning he and Anne sat on the sand watching the oystercatchers. Parent bird flew out to the reef (waves washing over), worked a mussel free, flew back to the sand above tide-mark, broke it open, dragged fish out, flew up to higher sand where the chick was sitting in, or walking around, the 'nest' (hardly more than a hollow with maybe a few twigs or sticks). Chick, well fed by this hour, accepted the mussel with bad grace. Parent bird returned to the reef for more. When finally the tide had covered the mussel bed, the parent bird went to the empty shells and lunched off scraps still adhering.

Time to close this notebook. Henry wonders idly whether, when the new term begins, he might take HOD's advice and turn his critical attention to the work of Hone Tuwhare.

Sex in America

T HIS IS THE MOMENT WHEN HE RELAXES. HE THINKS he may only have learned it recently – learned it consciously – and even now it doesn't always happen. It's when all the anxiety goes, and all the effort. He is no longer worrying whether he is pleasing her, whether she wants more or less, slower or faster, where they are going, when they will arrive. All of that deliberateness collapses and dissolves into this sense of the pleasure of it, body and mind that have become one, bathed in it, irradiated. There is nothing else he wants in the world, only this moment when he can stop like a rower resting on his oars, gliding between banks, listening, looking.

He is now that part – exclusively has become – *it*. Hooked in hard. Locked by her at base. Anchored. That's where his sense of himself is clearest. No boundary: himself as part of her; herself as part of him.

But no – not 'exclusively'. Not quite. Isn't he also most of his skin? A nose breathing her hair? Two eyes turning sideways to see the nameless couple on the big hotel bed in the big hotel mirror?

Seeing, yes – and recognising the self that is not-self, the voyeur, registering what it sees, taking private note of it. Remembering.

He meets her eyes in the mirror, half-answers her half-smile, her eyes looking, then rolling back as he moves slowly down and out, up and in, back into the lock.

She is small, perfectly made, laid out there on the sheets, one neat leg thrown wide and hanging off the bed. He likes that image which makes him look so large, over her, in her.

If they were talking about this moment rather than living it – if they should talk about it afterwards – he might say to her, naive, laid open and made innocent by the pleasure of it, that he wonders whether fucking is like this for many, or most, or few. Why should there be so many shadows over the land-scape, so many storms, so much violence? Why is the human world not full of benign and stupid sex-junkies, high and happy on their drug?

But they have not talked in that way – not in words; only in the language of skin and hair, textures, moistures, groans and sighs.

When, two days ago, he was woken in her apartment by her climbing over him, getting out of the bed, trying not to wake him, saying, 'Reste, mon ami. Ne bouge-pas' – because she had to go to work while he, the visitor, did not – he was not able to remember her name. While she was in the shower he scrabbled through her pocketbook to find it; and then didn't at once recognise it – Catherine Demas – because she pronounces it in French: 'Cutreen'.

'My Cutreen-Cunt,' he thought, lying there in her bed, the first morning after the first night, a cable car clanking by on the hill – trying to live it as if he, who has never been to Paris except in his mind, were Henry Miller, and she some wonder-fuck from *Quiet Days in Clichy*.

That first night there was more of the anxiety, the effort, the need to prove something (this was, in brother Greg's phrase, '*Sex in America*!'); less of the pleasure. Or rather, the pleasure was in the excitement – because it was happening – to him; because he was doing it, and well.

She has thrown her head sideways and is shuddering – once, a moment later a second time. These shudders are what she told him last night were her 'Leetle comings'. 'Ze beeg one' she likes to save up, hold off . . .

He responds to something, moves as she seems to require, and wonders how this can be, how it works, that already, like long-established dancing partners, some intuitive monitor in each feels what it makes the other feel – and responds.

But there is separateness too. He recognises it as he recalls, sees behind closed eyes, the sea lions among the wharf piles in the harbour at Monterey, lolling back in the green water, barking for scraps, and the huge pelican birds looking down at them – some part of his consciousness going randomly off on a track of its own, indifferent, and then puzzling at itself.

It is as if the mind were a series of shut doors any one of which he can choose to open and look into. Here are the sea lions. Here is the beautiful monastery on the hill. Here are the shade-trees, some species of pine, and the white sands at Carmel; or the barren slopes of Big Sur about which Henry wrote his only boring book.

And here, behind this door (she twists on him and it springs open of its own accord, slamming the others shut) are simply colours – greens and purples and plum-reds, strong, heavy, dark . . .

And there are thoughts. Thoughts about thoughts, about thinking, about not thinking. Thoughts about images. About time . . .

'Timeless', is the word that comes to him. And then a phrase – 'No yesterday. No tomorrow' – at once rejected (she has turned on her side like a swimmer, resting, and he adjusts the angle, slows the pace) because it belongs not to reality but to Hollywood. There *is* before; there *will be* after. Yesterday was the day of the Berkeley Campus, and Fisherman's Wharf, and the deer in the garden at Wildcat Canyon Road. Tomorrow will be whatever comes to fill the blank space that represents it. Today is now – this body-surfing, this skin-skimming, this cave-craving.

So why, in the midst of it, should he receive at precisely this moment, like a brief urgent interruption at once cut off, a sensation as if he were hearing screams and breaking glass? Is one of those mind-doors marked, 'Future: Enter at your own Risk'?

A few weeks back in a bar in Los Angeles he met a scientist – Austrian originally, now American. Otto Bergman. Theoretical physicist – his subject, Time. Otto talked about relativity. About (for example) how old you would be if you set off at age twenty and went through space and returned after one hundred earth-years. Tried to explain that, no, you would not be one hundred and twenty – then gave up and told it another way. (Or was it an unrelated anecdote?) Once when he was a child in Vienna, lying in the dark drifting towards sleep, he was jerked into full waking by the sound of the large single electric light fitting that hung in the centre of his bedroom crashing to the floor. He yelled in fright. His mother rushed in, turned on the light switch, and the light fitting crashed to the floor . . .

He leans back and without withdrawing puts one hand down where the curls of her pubic hair lightly brush his fingers and palm. Pleasure: the desire not to be other than this, and here, and now. Or rather, the absence of the desire to be other. The loss of ego in the discovery of self: 'Is it' (the question comes, he thinks, from *Moby Dick*?) 'I, God, or who, that lifts this arm?'

On the dressing table under, and reflected in, the mirror is the Manual. Why did he bring it on this journey? Glossy. Plastic. Hard and bright. Not those in-the-head velvety colours of sex. The pages perforated and slipped into place

110

over multiple wire hinges so its drug company information can be brought always up to date. Quick-fire, easy-to-use, for hard-pressed physician-subscribers.

In that little back room of the gallery where she showed him the Mirós two days ago, she asked was he a travelling salesman. It was the Manual – hated object – that prompted the question . . .

She is making strange sounds now, in the throat and between the lips – murmuring, twittering – in French, Esperanto, Desperato, Ecstatica. Her fingers going (so to speak) to the keyboard, going at it, scripting it, all action, the eye of her storm making precarious his control, her tongue forced suddenly, big and unmoving into his mouth. He does what he can with it, sucking on it hard as on a great lozenge . . .

He came (he told her in the little room among the Mirós) from a far country away to the south, down under the earth's curve, Ireland's matching state, you might say (some of his forebears were Irish) – much rain, many cows and no serpents. Travelled then, in his early twenties, to its nearest neighbour, notable for arid spaces and many serpents. Then, after some years, came here to America, and had still not, despite his best efforts in that neighbouring southern vastness, and more recently here in the Land of the Free and the Home of the Brave, seen a living snake – not until this day. The day of the snake. The day of the Mirós. The day of (he would forget her name, and find it on a card in her pocketbook while she sang in the shower her comic-gravel Piaf imitation, 'Je ne rrrregrrette rrrrien . . .') Catherine. Cutreen.

He had scored (it was a long story) a green card, scored a job working out of LA, and so rode in his company car the highways of the West Coast States – California, Oregon, Washington – and even inland through desert and canyon and mountain country, Arizona, New Mexico, Utah, Nevada, signing on medical men, supplying those who were already subscribers with the latest updates, collecting their annual subscriptions. He was no salesman, liking the desert routes best where there was least business, the strange, down-at-heel, off-the-main-highway motels, the red rocks, the more-than-mansize cacti holed by nesting birds, the coolness of morning in desert towns like Phoenix, their gardens under sprinklers in the clear dry early light.

And then there was Yosemite. Long ago and far away, as a child in that innocent dismal-distant home-place, listening to rain on the iron roof and seeing it fall on the green garden while registering also the intolerable melancholy of a bird that called itself the riro riro, he had read in *National Geographic* about Yosemite, looked at pictures of its steep rock-faces, its redwoods, its cabins under them by rushing water; had read, imagined, hunted there in his head, sat around campfires; had played it out to the hilt, until the invented stories lost, by dint of repetition, not their charm, but their power to remove, and so had been set aside in favour of stronger drugs. Set aside and forgotten.

So he came home to Yosemite as to a previous life. He didn't tire of driving through it. Whenever possible, even when it took him some distance out of his way, that was the route he chose.

The deserts too, and even the Grand Canyon, were landscapes out of a Western-addicted childhood. These were the territories where he had learned to ride and to shoot. Driving through them now, the Manual-man with the accent some thought was Boston, others (closer) identified as Crocodile Dundee's, he made unscheduled stops, wandered off the road among those cacti that looked like set-props left when the movie-making came to an end, turning stones over with his toe (public notices and the local lore warned against it) seeking sight of what was still denied. Scorpions, spiders, lizards, funghi – yes; but a snake – never! Was there upon him some spell, some reverse curse, the luck of the Irish which was the blessing of St Patrick, determining that where others saw serpents, and even sometimes died of their bite, he should see none?

Or not (he explained to her, his eyes sometimes on one or another of the Mirós, sometimes on her perfect upper lip) until this morning, the morning of this visit. He was to come up by air from LA, take the shuttle flight, a break from his work, his endless driving on the roads. He had a room booked in a hotel. He was to see *Parsifal* – that was his purpose, the one which circumstance, or more precisely *she*, would forestall – at the San Francisco Opera House. Ticket by courtesy of a satisfied customer, a lonely Las Vegas medic, lover of opera, fanatic of Wagner, who enjoyed talking to this bringer-of-the-Manual, and looked forward to his next visit (now it would be an embarrassment – or could he read up Wagner in a library and pretend?) when they could discuss the music, the drama of the king's wound, the king's bath, the holy spear, the magic chalice, and the sexual charms of (could he have said she was called?) *Kundry*!

So he was walking that morning down Pearl in Santa Monica to Lincoln Boulevard where the bus ran that would go all the way to the airport. In no hurry. Knowing it was early, and that the planes flew on the hour . . .

And there it was. Right there. Moving. Rippling along in the gutter, keeping pace with him. Bronze back, yellow sides, beady eye, flickering tongue. Not much more than a half metre in length. Not happy to be where it was, nor to have him watching it – and when it came to a car access it turned and made its way up from the roadway, slipping, hesitating, seeming to find the smooth concrete uncongenial, unhelpful to its means of locomotion. So he had time to take out his camera and photograph it – once, twice, a third time – before it reached the front garden of the house and slithered quickly away among low shrubs at the side of the drive.

She talks constantly of Paris, longs to return, is glad that he knows some French, can read it, even speak it a little, however haltingly; that he seems to understand her francophone jokes, her little obscenities; that Paris is high on the list of sacred places he plans to set foot in before (and that will be soon) he reaches 30 – the age when, for some reason no more explicable than why Cinderella should have to cut and run at midnight, he sees his *wanderjahre* coming to an end with a return to that green dark under-region of rain and cows.

Naked, they sprawl in her bed, on the rug beside it, on the divan in her sitting room; or sit in kimonas (she has one from a past lover that fits him) at the table in her kitchen drinking coffee, eating fruit yoghurt and croissants, looking out over the rooftops towards the bay where the morning fog is lifting, while much of her talk is of Paris, or of the means to get back there.

Yes France is home. Yes she can return at any time. But she plans to go with money, enough to open her own little gallery in Paris. Otherwise it will have to be the provinces, Dijon perhaps, or her home town of Mâcon, and that is not what she wants.

She tells him about the little Paris street she lived in when she was a student. The gravelled square at one end with the big church and the fountain and the two cafés with tables out on the pavements. The two bookshops, three picture galleries, the épicerie. The boulangerie on the corner half way up the cobbled street, where once (once only) she let the baker fuck her in return for a gâteau, trés grand, trés sculptural, for her boyfriend's birthday, and came home with puffs and handprints of flour on her quickly lifted skirt. And at the end of the street the palace and the fountains, and the extensive gardens so full of statuary you kept coming on some famous head or torso or figure you hadn't seen before, peering out of a clump of bushes or crouching among them, just when you thought you knew them all.

Then, embarrassed at having talked so much and with such enthusiasm, she asks him again to talk about *his* home. He tells her instead about Santa Monica, his apartment there not far from the sea – one long white room with kitchen and bathroom off – and how he has furnished it: at one end his 'office', a white-topped desk on white enamelled steel legs, a small black computer (company issue, for his records), three black shelves for books and CDs, red plastic trays for paper, a white phone and fax machine and black office chair. On the wall above the desk a pink-faced electric clock that advertises piston rings; and along the outer wall under a window, the red futon on which he sleeps.

That, he explains, is 'the working and sleeping end'; and when she frowns at this conjunction he explains that if she should visit LA, *when* she visits, the futon will be opened out to make a double bed, and everything on the desk will be shut down, the computer and fax machines switched off.

At the other end is his kitchen-eating-living space, with small dining table and chairs, divan with florid cushions, and two chairs in dark red canvas, DIRECTOR in black on the back of one, SCRIPT EDITOR on the other. This is the end where he eats, sits, watches television, and (very seldom) entertains.

Out there, through the windows, is his sandy back garden, watered daily, his small patch of lawn, with a lemon tree, and bougainvillea over the high enclosing fence.

And (turning to the left past the windows) the long blank wall on which he imagined the Miró . . .

Ah the Miró. 'Miroir de l'homme, II.' Her eyes light up. 'You will buy it. You will buy it, mon amour. Il faut, absolument. You must.'

She pushes him to the floor, and as he crawls away she throws a leg over, bestrides him, rides him around the room, tightening her knees on his naked flanks, asking can he feel what she calls, mixing French and English, her 'levers' kissing his back.

Suddenly he tips her sideways on to the rug and falls on her, pinning her down. 'What was it like with the baker?'

His plane left late. There had been an hour, more than an hour, while it had waited, fully loaded in the Los Angeles sun, for word that a backlog of planes stacked to come in through fog at San Francisco had reduced sufficiently for this one, heading there, to be cleared for takeoff.

When, after the delay and an hour's flight, they got there, the fog had lifted. He took the bus into town, checked in at his hotel, the Holiday Inn at the City Centre, made sure that he knew the route to the Opera House, then headed for Union Square.

He was strolling, looking for somewhere to sit down, drink coffee, read a newspaper, when the painting (if that was what it was) took his eye. It was in the window of a small art dealer just off the Square. There was a vivid central column, just off-vertical, rising as if from two mounds and ending in a sky containing streaks and puffs of bright colour that might have been fireworks or fantastic clouds. He did not know what kind of art work it was, what technique it exemplified, only that its strange mixture of billowing unbounded colour and fine hard dark ink-lines excited him, and that he imagined it (not 'seriously', not thinking of himself as a person who 'buys works of art') hanging on that emptiness of white wall which had seemed, the better he made his apartment look, the more to demand that it be adorned with something bright and bold.

He looked at the work, enjoyed, moved on, returned,

noticed a detail: around the base of the colour-column a small serpent curled, its eye black, its forked tongue flame-red as if the mouth were filled with fire.

It was not the name, Miró, which he now saw at the bottom corner beside the date, 1970, but the serpent – that fortuitous conjunction with what he had seen only a few hours before in Santa Monica – which made him step into the gallery guessing he must look as he felt, tentative . . .

There, however, to be greeted reassuringly by a young woman – strong French accent, small neat good looks, a manner that mixed neutral practicality and unobtrusive charm.

The Miró, she told him, was one of a series. Number 66 of 250. The technique, aqua-tint and dry-point. As for the form (she was talking as she removed it from the window) – phallic obviously, wasn't it so?

And he saw now that the central column ended in a kind of arrowhead; while the two mounds it rose from might have been symbolic testes.

'Maybe about the Fall,' she suggested. 'It's called "Miroir de l'homme, II".'

She took him into a small back room, closed the door, and hung the picture under perfect lighting. She brought out other Mirós to place beside it for comparison; showed him documents of authentication which came from a dealer in New York; opened books on Miró and showed how 'Miroir de l'homme, II' was characteristic of the artist's last phase; talked about recent Miró prices in London and Paris, and suggested they were higher there; told him she had a client whose way of financing his summer holiday in Europe was to buy a minor work by a major Modernist here on the West Coast, and sell it in London, Paris or Madrid.

Somewhere in all of this a price was mentioned, $3750, though she thought her employer, the owner of the gallery, might consider a lower offer that was not unreasonable.

In some part of his mind he was trying to disentangle his interest in the painting from his interest in the woman. Before this moment he would have said he did not have $3750 to spend on a work of art. Not even one thousand. But why not? He was employed, and saving. He would have spent that much – more – on a car, and only did not because the company supplied one. This might even be a profitable investment, if the Frenchwoman was to be believed . . .

It was late afternoon. When they emerged from the small room, the gallery was closed, the staff had gone. He said he would now have to go away and think seriously.

'Ah mon ami,' she said, shaking her head. 'Thinking is not so good as doing. In this art business you must strike . . . what do you say in English? While it is hot?'

While it was hot, he struck. He asked her to let him take her to a restaurant where they could continue to talk about it. He was surprised when she accepted; and there was even a moment of regret about *Parsifal*, which he would now not see.

That night and the next he spent at her apartment. The third, because she had a friend coming through town to whom she had promised a bed for the night, they went to his hotel. The day after that he was to return to LA.

The storm (his and hers) is passing, passes, is passed. The big hard lozenge has been removed from his mouth. They roll apart, holding hands, legs (his left, her right) still interlocked, murmuring, staring up at the ceiling which is dimly lit by a single bedside lamp. They drift into sleep.

Later they half wake, pull covers over one another, re-arrange legs and arms, switch off the lamp, kiss as sexlessly as sister and brother, and sleep again.

After how long – one hour? three? – he is dreaming of *Parsifal*, the opera he has not seen, when the characters' singing changes, becomes shrieking, screaming. Something is shattering. Now it is a scene in the movie of *Dr Zhivago* when a sheet of ice that has filled the open door of a railway wagon is smashed. No, not ice. Glass. And the voices – yelling. Calling for help . . .

'Chéri.' She is speaking into his ear – he can feel her hair against his cheek. 'Réveille-toi. Wake, darling.'

She shakes him gently. He can hear sirens now. 'Something is happening.'

'Some sing is 'upning?' he says, imitating her.

They are on the eighth floor and their room is in darkness, but light comes in from outside. Naked, they go to the window. There is a fire in the next-door hotel, the San Franciscan. It seems to be on the floor exactly opposite theirs, and the one above. Elevators are not working and fire has cut access by the stairs, trapping those in the two top floors who have not already escaped. Corridors are filling with smoke. People are shouting down into the street, some unfurling useless ropes of knotted sheets. In a room directly opposite a man, very calm, very orderly, goes to the window and looks down, goes to the door and looks out into the smoke-filled corridor, picks up the phone and speaks, sorts things in his room, returns to the window and looks down where two ladder trucks have arrived.

The ladders ascend. Soon rows of dark huddled figures are climbing out on to their platforms, helped by firefighters. Some people have to be encouraged, even forced, but the line keeps moving. There is less noise now as they clamber down the eight or nine floors to the street. Other firefighters wearing masks are up there with hoses. Some appear to have the job of breaking every window on the two top floors. Panes, smashed out, crash down to a street now full of police cars, firetrucks, ambulances, and a small late-night crowd held back behind a police line. There are shouts of encouragement, cheers, flash-lights.

He stands behind her at the window and feels her begin to push back against him, moving from side to side. He looks down. She is leaning forward, legs apart, arms forward, propping against the sill. The vaguely diffused light from the night city gleams on the perfect white curve of her buttocks. She turns her head to look at him. She is like some lovely animal. 'Do it, mon vieux,' she says.

He tries, spreading his feet wide, bending at the knees, but his legs are too long. He can't quite get in under, and up.

On the floor there are two books of the San Francisco telephone directory. She moves them into place and stands on them. 'Now,' she says. 'Do it.'

He does. Flames are licking out through the smashed window of what was the orderly man's room. He sees fire through the wild aureole of her hair. The smell of smoke has begun to reach into their room. Shouts come up from the street, where the whirling lights of the firetrucks spiral round and round. Glass continues to crash down. Men dressed as for a space-walk can be seen moving from room to room, in and out of patches of light. Someone still left on the top floor yells for help, and the spacemen turn and look at one another and lumber off in the direction of the cry.

'Harder,' she says. 'Harder!'

He drives up into her with more force, grunting, thighs slapping upward against buttocks and the back of her legs. She is lifted with the force of each thrust.

'Harder,' she says.

Next morning they had room service bring them an early breakfast. He was looking in the paper for news of the fire when she said, 'Mon cher, today you must confirm.'

'Confirm?'

'The purchase, darling. The Miró.'

'Ze pur-chase duh-leeeng.'

She cuffed his head. 'Don't imitate me. I'm serious. You must sign the paper. Put down a deposit.'

He rolled over and looked at her. 'I can't buy the Miró.'

'Why not? You like it. You want it.'

'I don't have the money.'

'I don't believe you.'

'Well, let's say I have it but I need it.' He saw her expression and decided to make it clear. 'I mustn't accumulate . . . *things*. That's all. I'm on the road, Honey.'

'You could make a profit.'

'If I sold. But would I? I don't know the market, the dealers . . . Look, I've thought about it, carefully. The Miró's lovely. But not for me. Not this time.' In case there should be doubt he added, 'That's final, Catherine. It has to be.'

It was as if she had been shot out of the bed by the release of a spring. Naked, her face set hard in an expression he had not seen before, she fumbled to put on her bra. 'So it was all a lie.'

'What was a lie?'

'All this.' She waved a hand at the bed that was like a battlefield. 'All this fucking me . . .'

Silence, until he said, in a voice that sounded strained and weak, 'You mean you fucked me so I would . . .'

She was not listening. She had found her underpants. Now she dragged her skirt over them. The face was still hard, but there were tears. 'You are not a man of honour.'

'A man of . . . Jesus. Did you think I was the baker? Did you fuck me for a "cake"?'

Silence. She had dragged her shirt on and was tucking it in, roughly so there were creases and lumps. She went to the mirror to look at her tears and touch them with her finger.

'What do you get for making a sale, Catherine? A commission? Ten percent?'

No answer.

'Is that what you're worth? Ten percent of three seven five zero? 375 bucks? For three days of heavy sex? One two five a night? Is that how I'm supposed . . .'

He got out of bed, his movements expressing indignation, displaying it. In his travel bag he found his chequebook. He went to the table and wrote her the cheque. He held it out to her. 'Take it.'

She was standing looking down at it. He did not think of it as the payment of a debt – did not really expect that she would accept it. It was a way of making clear to her . . .

She took it, read the figures, folded it, and tucked it into her pocketbook.

He had a window seat. Down there the arid landscape of Southern California rolled and lifted away towards the mountains, with here and there startling green patches where irrigation water had been pumped in from the north. Through the windows on the opposite side he caught the broad glare of afternoon sunlight striking off the ocean. They had begun the long descent into Los Angeles.

His tray table was down and there was a postcard lying on it. He had addressed it, and written 'Dear Greg'.

Greg was the brother who had sent a card saying all was well, life was boring, the Government was going to fall, and 'tell me about *Sex in America*!'

He remembered what she had said when he asked, 'What was it like with the baker?'

The baker, she had said, was nice. But he was – not old, but not a young man either, and they had done it standing up in the back of the shop. When it was over he had slumped to the floor and removed his tall white baker's hat. She had never seen him without it. He was bald, and there were beads of sweat shining on his brow.

''e was very nice,' she said. 'Very sympathique, zat bak-aire.

122

But I would never let 'im do it again. I was afraid I might kill 'im.'

In small neat spider-letters he wrote on the card, 'Have just spent three beautiful nights with a beautiful French mercenary. Won't see her again. Thought I was after (your phrase) *Sex in America*. Feel now as if I'm in love. Can you explain that, mon vieux?'

Figures of Speech

SHORTLY AFTER MY SIXTY-THIRD BIRTHDAY I STOOD ON – and in – a machine outside the New Life Superstore in the Doubleday Grand National Shopping Mall somewhere, I am no longer sure exactly where, in the United States. I was travelling, as aging academics do, talking, as they do, about my subject, literature at large, poetry in particular. I put in the required coins, and the machine, telling me first to stand straight, then eyeing me with a red beam, printed out my height and weight, in metrics and in the older measures. That these facts came together with a print-out of the date and time, even to the hour and minute, gave what might be the most precisely recorded moment of my biography, should anyone care to write it – and I hasten to affirm that, to this late date, there has not been the least reason why anyone should.

What it told me was:

> Weight – 79.4 kg / 175 lb
> Height – 1.84 m / 6ft $\frac{1}{2}$ in

Below there was a line showing the 'Ideal Weight (depending on Constitution)' for a person of that height:

Man		
Light	Medium	Heavy
76.8 kg / 169 lb	80.3 kg / 177 lb	85.2 kg / 188 lb

It looks almost perfect; at the very least satisfactory. For a six-foot male (which is to say tall in the 1950s, medium tall in the 1990s) of 'light' constitution, I was a little overweight, about what you would expect for one of my age who walks a lot, doesn't pant going up hills, and can still (briefly – say for a few hundred yards, or even metres) run like an imitation of the runner he once was.

These are the facts. But the truth is not quite (and when is it ever?) caught by them; and it was this hidden discrepancy that set me thinking about Claudia Strange. It was in those late 1950s years, when I was tall rather than (as now) medium tall, that I knew Claudia as a friend. That was in England where we had each come, she from the United States, I from New Zealand, as postgraduate students.

'Friend' is exactly right, as in 'just good friends'– meaning 'only' and 'no more than'. I would have liked more; but Claudia had a preference, a predilection, even (it doesn't seem too much to say) a passion, for men who were, on the New Life Superstore machine's simple scale, 'Heavy'. Not 'Heavy' in the sense of fat. Claudia's men had to be big; they had to bulk large; but it had to be hard bulk. It was as if she wanted to be crushed by an excess maleness.

Other things were important. Brain was important. Personality, wit, sensibility, imagination, social skills. A man who wanted to interest her had to have them all. She had no wish to be dominated, oppressed, extinguished. It was only that if a man was to arouse her romantic side and her sexual passion (and we were at an age when the two are only distinguished with difficulty), these excellent personal and social qualities had to be amply housed. They had to inhabit a large strong frame.

Which is why the New Life Superstore's print-out made me think of her. Most of my life I have been a string bean – a *strong* string bean, ego demands I should add. I was athletic, healthy, a very large eater – but thin, gaunt, even (I am trying to see myself as she would have seen me) emaciated. At 15 I was already six foot and weighed in for school boxing at under 150 pounds. Thirty years later my height and weight were the same. I was a fat person's dream of success. But (and such is the nature of human perversity) for most of my adult life I yearned, as I put it to my family, to 'achieve fatness'.

I achieved it, or achieved it by my own poor standard of bulk, only in my 50s, by which time Claudia Strange was long-dead, and famous.

There's a scene I remember very clearly which I think catches something about the arcane nature of our friendship. Claudia was visiting me in London where I was doing research in the British Museum, and we were walking in a long narrow park which (at least in my recollection of it) runs north from Kensington High Street somewhere west of the lane off Phillimore Gardens where I occupied a bedsit. It was a time when nannies could still be seen about that area in large numbers, walking their charges in prams and pushchairs; and by my observation they divided into two distinct types – the round-hatted uniformed professional English kind, hard-faced relics of what was even then a past age, who gathered at the Round Pond in Kensington Gardens; and the stylish young au pairs, mostly French, who were to be seen in this little park close to what had become my home.

In those days I had girlfriends, any number of them. Even my foolish and self-mocking obsession with Claudia Strange didn't prevent that; and there was one of these French nannies who had taken my fancy and who seemed, though I hadn't yet spoken to her, to be encouraging the interest I let her see she aroused. On this particular day I took Claudia with me so she could see and comment on the young Frenchwoman; also, perhaps, so the young Frenchwoman could see me with a nice-looking American girl.

It was part of what seems, when I look back on it, an

elaborate game Claudia and I played. I suppose I wanted to arouse her jealousy; and I even believe I did arouse it – or, if it wasn't jealousy, it was at least possessiveness. She would say to me, looking at some young woman I pointed out in a library or at a party, 'Yes, she's perfect, Carlo. Go for it.' But I always felt she did it knowing that that was not what I really wanted. And my tardiness, my failure to go into action as long as she was there to entertain me, pleased her, reinforcing the confidence it gave her to know that I was in love with her. Claudia didn't want me; but nor was she quite ready or willing to give me up.

But on this particular day the young French nanny never appeared. We found a park bench and sat waiting for her, watching others of her kind, giving them marks out of ten, making literary jokes and weak puns. And at some point in this aimless verbal tennis which we both loved to play, I used the word 'skinny'. Perhaps I said, touching the old wound, that of course this Frenchwoman wouldn't want me as a boyfriend; like Claudia she would find me too skinny.

Her reaction was strange. I don't think it was that she had never heard the word – though I do remember she told me that in America it would be much more common to say scrawny. But the way I had said it delighted her because, she told me, I had *screwed up my nose*! She got me to say it again – and again. Over and over I had to screw up my nose and say it: 'Skinny.'

Was she mocking me? I don't think so. It was almost as if, just for a moment, she was in love with me. What is certainly true is that from that moment on I could usually please Claudia, catch her attention, make her laugh, win her back from a displeasure or a sulk, almost, even, if only for a moment, make her love me, simply by reminding her that I was *skinny*.

Claudia, I should explain, was a scientist, a graduate in

physics who had come to England to do a postgraduate degree at Cambridge. But she had been one of those brilliant, and rare, students who shine almost equally at arts and sciences and have difficulty choosing between them. She had loved studying literature, and still liked to read good books and talk about them. She found most of her fellow science students unappealing. The men, she said, were too narrow – either ignorant of the arts, or interested (the mathematicians, usually) only in classical music. As for the women (and there were very few in science in those days) – she dismissed them as an unstylish lot, with big legs and no makeup, whose idea of a good time was singing 'Green grow the rushes-oh', or 'No more double-bunking', around a fire in a tramping club hut. 'Weedy' for the men, 'dowdy' for the women – those were her words, and that was her summing up of her colleagues. It's not surprising that many of them spoke more or less slightingly of her after her death.

Claudia and I got to know one another first by correspondence, and that, as I will explain, was unfortunate. She kept a journal – highly literate, clever, witty, brisk and unbridled – the entries accompanied by excellent black and white sketches; and it was a small section of this journal, just a few pages dealing with her journey by sea from New York to London, that appeared in a universities literary magazine to which I contributed two poems. I was struck by what she had written. It leapt off the page, slightly breathless, the words and impressions spilling out and tripping over one another, but vivid, lucid, spontaneous, full of energy and colour. The notes on contributors mentioned her College, and on an impulse, a quite untypical one, I wrote to tell her how much I had enjoyed her contribution.

Back by return post came a letter. I have it here on my desk as I write. 'Very bad form of me,' it begins, 'not giving you a moment to catch your breath, but I'm firing a note straight back to tell you what an immense kick it gave me that someone, a contemporary and student of literature (and a poet to boot – a real one!) should not only like my journal extract, but like it enough to find words for why, words quite wise and carefully weighed, and should even be generous enough to put pen to paper and stamp to envelope . . .'

So it rattled on. That was Claudia's way. She told me about herself, where she came from, what she was doing in Cambridge. She wrote warmly about my poems. I was charmed, as I had been by the journal, and wrote back. Our correspondence continued for seven or eight weeks before our first meeting, and in that time more than a dozen letters went back and forth.

By now I was truly interested in her, keen (as she was) that we should meet. We had exchanged photographs and I could see she was at the very least pretty, perhaps beautiful. She, I suppose, could see that I had eyes, nose, mouth, teeth, hair, all in reasonable proportion and the right relation one to another.

As for our minds, these had already met on the page and liked each other, even when there were differences of opinion. So now we could get on and like each other in reality.

Neither of us could know, of course, what other lovers, potential or actual, already existed. In my case there were a few, none of them very serious. In hers, since she was an attractive and clever young woman at the University of Cambridge, where men outnumbered women ten to one, my potential competitors were an army. But since Claudia responded as positively to my letters as I did to hers, the omens were propitious, and disappointment lay in wait for us both.

That autumn I bought my first car. It was a Ford Popular, grey, unstylish, tall on its thin wheels, flat-footed on its unyielding springs, and it cost me £450 new. I looked out at it, parked in the mist under a street-lamp in the narrow lane outside my bedsit, half-pleased, half-alarmed at what I had done. I had no licence to drive, and no immediate prospect of getting one. This, I think, had something to do with the Suez Crisis. The queue of new car-owners waiting to be tested was long, and meanwhile I was supposed to drive only with a licence-holder beside me.

One afternoon, on an impulse, I removed the large red 'L' from my front and back bumpers and set off, unlicensed and unaccompanied, for Cambridge. First there was the problem of getting out of London – nothing like as difficult as it would be now, but for a learner driver, a nightmare nonetheless. There was no M11 in those days, and I can see, looking at a road map which might be the one I used all that long time ago, that once clear of the outskirts of the city I must have ambled north through Harlow, Bishop's Stortford and Great Chesterfield.

I remember there was a part of the journey when the charm of rural England swept over me – a charm which, for one of my colonial background and education, was always powerful. It was the 'season of mists and mellow fruitfulness', and so much of what I saw had literary echoes, as if the showering orange woods, the discreet streams and hills, the cropped fields and thatched villages, had come into existence as illustrations of famous books and poems rather than the other way about. And this excitement merged with the pleasure of being free of claustrophobic London, and with the prospect of meeting the young American woman whose letters and photograph had taken such a grip on my imagination.

But as I drove the autumn mist got thicker and, near Cambridge, while the afternoon closed down towards dark, became fog. British fogs in those days (it was before the Clean Air Act, or before it had begun to have an effect) were unimaginably thick, and by the time I reached the outskirts of Cambridge I was stopping every few hundred yards and walking up the road in the weak beams of the Ford Popular's lights, so I could be sure what was out there ahead of me.

Somehow I found Claudia's College, and the house nearby where she lived with other American and Commonwealth students who, like her, were already graduates. Enquiring for her there I was directed to a nearby pub. When I walked in I recognised her at once, sitting at a table with a group of young women and one or two men. She was dressed in a way which I remember seemed, though I'm no longer sure why, distinctly American. She was wearing a neat brown jacket with a matching skirt (I think she would have called it a 'costume') and a yellow shirt. Her hair, thick and golden brown, was quite long and softly wavy. Her eyes were blue and keen. She wore bright lipstick which, when she laughed, framed two perfect rows of strong, white, evenly spaced teeth. There was a general look of being well-groomed. She had submitted (as the poet Yeats would have said) 'to the discipline of the looking-glass'. And there was in her manner the impression of one eager to please, or to make an impression.

Claudia saw me staring at her, failed to recognise me, and when she looked a second time and my eyes were still on her, gave me the kind of glare a confident woman gives to a stranger whose attentions are unwelcome.

Hungry and thirsty after my difficult drive, I bought a pint and a pie and sat at a table near the door, where I could keep her in my sights without staring.

Half an hour later she got up to leave. As she passed I tugged at her sleeve. 'I'm sorry if I seemed to stare,' I told her. 'I didn't want to interrupt your conversation. You don't recognise me?'

I had stood up to greet her. She took the hand I held out to her, holding it absent-mindedly while she looked hard at me – at my eyes, my face, my hair, my thin shoulders and narrow waist. 'You're not . . . Carlo?'

I expected recognition would be followed by one of those broad smiles I had seen her unleashing at her companions around the table. Instead there was a frown. Her mouth closed tight. Her eyes flashed anger. I'm not even sure she didn't stamp her foot on the floor. What did I mean by coming unannounced? I should have let her know, not just burst in on her life like this. She was busy. It was the worst of bad form. It was intolerable . . .

I said I was sorry. I was already backing away from her, taking my coat from the chair where I had thrown it, making for the door. In part what I felt was guilt. Because there wasn't time to reflect, I behaved as if I had indeed done wrong. But already there was another part of me that was saying, *This is a madwoman.*

I found my way to my car, got in and drove out of Cambridge, without any certainty about whether I was heading north or south. The fog persisted, and soon brought me to a halt. I drove off the road on to a flat gravelly surface. Getting out I could see rocks looming over me.

There was no heater in the car, the seats were narrow, stiff-backed and hard. I curled up into a ball on the back seat, pulling my overcoat tight around me, and tried to sleep. I would have said I didn't sleep at all, only dozed, but in the morning I was woken by a tapping on the driver's window. I leaned forward and wound it down. The fog now was on the inside of the glass. Out there it had cleared. A policeman was peering in at me.

Of course, I thought, this is how it *would* end. He was going to ask to see my licence, discover I was only a learner . . . I began to prepare my defence. I was not, when apprehended ('May it please your Honour') actually *driving* . . .

'I'm sorry, sir,' he said (in those days if you owned a car you were 'sir'). 'I just wanted to be sure you weren't dead.'

I confirmed that I wasn't, and climbed out. I had parked, I

now saw, in a kind of gravel pit. 'It didn't seem safe to drive last night,' I explained.

He was already back astride his bicycle. 'Very wise, I'd say, sir.' And he wobbled away over the rough surface, stopping to adjust the clips that held his trousers tight at the ankles before disappearing down the road.

My limbs were stiff. I was hungry, unshaven. I was also, by now, angry, and I remained angry all of that morning as I made my way back into London. That, I told myself, was the end of Claudia fucking Strange. Damn her! What a hellhound! What a bitch! There would be no more cosy letters. She could die, for all I cared. (And so on.)

But I think even while inwardly I raged, I knew (and I suppose it added to my rage) that by behaving in that uncivil way she had not really wiped out the fascination she held for me. She might even have added to it. Seeing her sitting with friends around a table, watching her talking, leaning forward, making an impression and knowing that she was, being in some indefinable way *American*, I think I had felt faintly disappointed, as if she was going to be less interesting than her letters. Her outburst had changed all that. Her anger with me had been inexplicable and outrageous. But it was as if she had proved herself. She was not just clever (in those days most women who got to a university were clever); she was also complex, intense, mysterious, and unpredictable. To wipe her from my consciousness, to have nothing more to do with her, which I was now quite determined to achieve, was not going to be easy.

My recollection is that when I got back to London there was already a letter from her, waiting for me. I don't see how that could have been possible. But certainly the letter, which I still have, was written that same night of our encounter, and reached me almost at once. She was, she said, 'truly sorry'. She sent me 'huge and abject apologies'. I had taken her by surprise, but that, she acknowledged, was no excuse. She wasn't able to explain her behaviour. She was like that (she went on) – 'badly behaved, given to rages'. Her middle names were 'Sturm' and 'Drang'.

'Life keeps taking me by surprise, and I don't act well. It's like when someone comes into a room and you don't hear them and you get a fright and jump – and maybe shout angrily – do you do that?' And then she gave up explanations. 'Oh God, my Carlo, what can I say to you to make amends? I squirm. I grovel. I die. Forgive me!'

My Carlo? This was new.

Almost at once I could feel my determination not to see her again dissolving. It wasn't masochism – I had no appetite for being knocked about by a strong woman; it was more like simple curiosity; fascination; *attraction.*

I tried not to write back, but it lasted no more than three or four days – and if I am honest I might have to say it lasted only two. Soon we were exchanging letters as if nothing had happened. She came down to London. We sat staring at one another across a table in a Lyons Teashop while she explained to me in a voice that quivered with intensity that she valued me, that she wanted us to be friends ('for life' was what she said), but that we could not be lovers – that was something I must accept and must not argue with. It could not be explained because it was, she said, inexplicable. Simply, it was so.

Later, when we knew one another well (and by this time the game of describing myself as 'skinny' had been discovered) she tried to explain why there had been that outburst at our first meeting. She was a great letter writer, and liked to exchange at least brief notes with her friends, even sometimes with men she saw every day in the lab. On paper, she said, people revealed the way their minds worked – something that wasn't always so clear when their physical presence dominated your consciousness. And by this measure I had been 'simply perfect'. There was never a word, or a phrase, or an image, that gave her the kind of sinking feeling, the sense of crushing disappointment, that sooner or later came with every other person she had ever known. But this had led her to build up a physical image of me that was wrong.

Trying to soften her explanation a little she assured me that it was nothing to do with 'good looks'. I had 'a nice, friendly, intelligent face'. What it had to do with was *size*. She had built up in her head an image of me as a large man – what I suppose would be called these days a hulk – and this had been so powerful, my bean-pole frame had presented itself to her as if it belonged to an imposter. It was as if I, the faultless letter-writer, had, after all, made a *mistake*. Of course she had no choice but to accept that the image before her and not the one in her head belonged to the man who had written my letters; but at that first moment of shock and, I suppose, disappointment (though she didn't use the word), it had made her angry.

So we were to be friends, not lovers; and for a time I developed a private life in which there was always a girlfriend, as they were called in those days, but also a friend – and it was the friend I was in love with. It wasn't long before I was loving Claudia with an absurd devotion, all the more painful because of my growing conviction, never confirmed by her and therefore never held by me with absolute certainty, that there were times, moments, when she loved me almost as much.

There was a Cambridge scholar, a fellow of Queen's, who had seen an article I had published and had written saying he knew a good deal about my area of research and would be happy to talk to me. It had been a kind offer, but at a time when I hadn't felt in need of help, and I had done nothing about it. Now I replied, and began visiting him. We used to stroll in the College garden – I remember his key to it looked like a small tennis racquet and was pushed horizontally into the lock – talking about my research; and I'm sure he wondered why, having taken the trouble to come so far, I was always so anxious to get away. One day, shortly after I had left him saying I had urgent work to do in the library before returning to London, he saw me sitting in a teashop with Claudia. We were holding hands across the table, looking into one another's eyes. After that my visits to talk with him were a little less friendly, and soon tapered off.

Holding hands in public might have been supposed to signal a lot more was going on in private, but with us that wasn't the case. Much has been written about Claudia's love life, and though I have my own opinions, and my own small areas of certain knowledge, it is not my intention either to add to or subtract from what has been said on that subject. In one of the two biographies that have been written of her I am not mentioned at all; in the other I am confused and conflated with a young man, an American she befriended on the liner from New York to London. So if the question whether Claudia and I were ever lovers should be asked I am content, since no simple answer would be adequate, to leave it unanswered – a matter of semantics rather than one of fact. We held hands in teashops. We kissed our greetings and farewells. There were times when we shared a bed – chastely, as she intended, but not (how shall I put it?) absolutely, or infallibly, or entirely. Let it be left there; because the important, or significant, truth is that we were never lovers in the wholehearted, fullblooded sense; and that was because she did not want us to be. Yet I am sure it would have happened. We were approaching it; we were almost there, when Jack Gibbs appeared on the scene.

Claudia and I were born ten days apart in the same year, but on either side of the line dividing Librans from Scorpios. I, whose professional life was to be devoted to works of the imagination, scorned the idea that our fates were ruled by the stars; she, the scientist, talked as if she considered it a hypothesis as reasonable as any other. Its efficacy, she suggested once, might be said to be demonstrated by our respective temperaments. I, the Libran, was the balanced person, mild-mannered, reasonable, equable. She, the Scorpio, was the one who carried a gun in what she called her pocketbook. She could kill someone she saw as an enemy, or even 'just anyone – if I was angry enough.' The scorpion was so deadly, she went on, it was capable even of stinging itself to death.

I thought her saying she carried a gun was only an image, a metaphor, part of the joke, but I was wrong. It was on the holiday we took together to Paris (the biographies, relying on the letters she wrote home to her sister, say she went alone) that I discovered she meant it literally. We had taken separate rooms but were lying together on a bed in one of them, recovering from a day's sightseeing, waiting to go out for our evening meal. Claudia was reading tourist material, planning what we would do the next day, when I read out to her our horoscopes in a newspaper. I don't remember quite how the conversation went from there; only that she joked again about being a dangerous Scorpio; and then playfully, but taking me utterly by surprise, she pulled out the small handgun and pointed it at my temple. 'Would you die for love, Carlo?' she asked. 'Of course you wouldn't. You're a Libran.'

I leapt off the bed, tripping in the narrow space between bed and window, and falling to the floor. 'It's all right,' she said, putting it away. 'Don't panic. There's a safety catch.'

Still on my knees I asked why on earth she kept such a thing. She said, 'Because I dislike it that my life's ruled by fear.'

I'd had such a fright I said no more for the moment, but that evening, when we stopped on a wide wooden footbridge over the Seine to look upriver at the floodlit walls and spires of Notre Dame, I suggested she should throw the gun away. 'Do it now,' I said. 'Get rid of it. Drop it into the river.'

We were leaning on the rail, and she took it out, turned it over in her hand, and held it over the water. For a moment I thought she meant to do it; but then she put it back in her bag and walked on.

The anger I'd felt at being frightened, and which I had suppressed, burst out now. 'For God's sake,' I barked at the back of her head. 'You don't need that thing. It's insane. Throw it away.'

But to seem to command Claudia was always a mistake. She turned to face me, blazing. Who did I think I was? Did I think I had the right to tell her what to do, how to live her life?

And who did she think *she* was? I responded, carrying an illegal weapon, threatening people.

As we crossed the remainder of the bridge I kept on at her. She fell into a grim silence, and then suddenly, as we went down the steps to the street, she turned, blazing again. 'Find yourself a nice sane safe girl, Carlo. Get on with your nice safe boring literary life, and let me get on with mine.' And she walked away from me, fast, disappearing down a narrow crowded street.

I let her go. Then I regretted it, and went looking for her around the streets where we'd intended to choose a restaurant. When I couldn't find her, I returned to our hotel. She wasn't there. Worried now, I walked all the way back to the Left Bank and wandered the streets again. It must have been nearly midnight before I stumbled into a café and ordered something very ordinary, a pizza, or a croque monsieur – not at all the gourmet feast we'd been planning to have together.

That night I left the door of my room unlocked and at two or three in the morning she came in and sat on the edge of my bed. She talked happily about where she had been, what she'd seen and done; about the Frenchman, a photographer, met in a bar, who had taken her in a taxi to see his studio somewhere near Montmartre. They had eaten couscous in a local restaurant and drunk a bottle of wine, and she had smoked one of his Gauloises, which had made her feel sick. I must have felt it all deeply, because I remember it as if I had been there.

There was no reference to our quarrel. It was as though it had never happened. I was baffled, helpless, angry with her, jealous of the photographer, suspicious about what might have happened, yet unwilling to show any of this because I was afraid of losing her again. I asked myself was I simply weak, and answered (a good Libran's balanced and fair assessment of the case!) that I was not inherently so, but that my position with her rendered me helpless. She was (the phrase came to me again) *a madwoman*, and I was in love with her.

While she talked she removed her outer garments and, in pants and bra, climbed into bed beside me. I thought perhaps she wanted to make love to me as an act of contrition, but I was wanting real love, not sex; or rather, I wanted them both, the one because of the other, and I kept well to my side of the bed.

I was wide awake now, and we went on talking. I had been remembering her saying that she carried a gun because she disliked it that her life was ruled by fear, and I asked what she had meant, what she was afraid of.

'Of dying,' she said. And then, after a moment, 'Not just of dying. Other things too. Everything. Nothing. Myself.'

She told me how at the age of fourteen or fifteen she had been troubled and depressed by thoughts of infinity – for example that our whole cosmos might be only a molecule in the knee of a giant who was himself as insignificant in his universe as we are in ours; and that conversely, there might be a whole minute universe locked away in a single atom. Infinity of space and time were horrifying enough. But infinity of scale had seemed to her the final horror. Thoughts of this kind, she said, had turned her towards science. But science hadn't really helped. Scientists shut their minds to everything but what was (I remember her phrase) 'proximate and measureable'. She'd come to the conclusion that there was no escape from her own thought processes – 'brainstorms', she called them. 'I just have to suffer them.'

'So you resort to astrology,' I said.

She reached over in the bed, feeling for me in the dark, finding my neck and running her fingers up into my hair. 'You don't understand me at all, do you Carlo?'

It was Jack Gibbs who rescued me from Claudia, and I did not (and I suppose do not, though I should) thank him for it. He was the hulk of her dreams – six foot three, handsome, broad-shouldered, strongly built, articulate, a top scientist, a 'two cultures' man, well read and with wide intellectual interests. He was four or five years her senior, had graduated from Cambridge, done postgraduate research in America, and was now back on his home turf, appointed to a senior position in the laboratory where she was working towards her doctorate.

I thought of him as Antony to her Cleopatra, and I used to comfort myself with lines from that play, saying to myself, for example, that I should not lament my loss,

> *But let determined things to Destiny*
> *Hold unbewailed their way.*

Jack eclipsed me. He eclipsed everyone in Claudia's firmament. She went for him, went at him, and told me all about it, not out of malice or to make me unhappy, but

141

blindly, because she needed to tell someone, and that need made her unaware of the pain it gave me to have to hear about it. I found her fierce focus on him, her sense of purpose, terrifying; and I remember joking about it, telling her that it put me in mind of an example, under the heading 'Figures of Speech', in my fifth form English Grammar book, illustrating the pun: 'Three strong girls went for a tramp. The tramp died.'

But Jack Gibbs was not going to die. He was the first to recognise in Claudia Strange not only a competent scientist but a brilliant one. Perhaps for him, at least during those first few years of their association, she fulfilled a dream almost as much as he fulfilled one for her.

Jack, now Professor Sir Jack Gibbs, has had a hugely successful career – how could it be otherwise for a scientist who won a Nobel Prize while still in his thirties? Yet it is Claudia whose biography has been written (twice); and it is Jack who has figured in her life story as a kind of demon. He used her, it has been said. Her work and not his own was crucial to the discoveries that earned him his prizes and his fame.

I am no scientist and don't pretend to understand anything of the intricacies of their work together; but on the face of it, and little as I care about Jack, I should say at once that those attacks are unfair. If Jack used Claudia it was because she wanted to be used, and was grateful for it. He was the first, the only one, to recognise her real potential and to employ it towards ends beyond the mere attainment of a PhD. And furthermore, we know how important her contribution was only because Jack took the trouble to make it known.

Shortly after her death (and that, remember, happened long ago – around the time of the assassination of President Kennedy) Jack wrote a long magazine article recounting how he and Claudia had spent weeks together going over the theoretical implications of his experimental work. Without her brilliant and penetrating analysis, he acknowledged, it would have taken him much longer, many years longer, to arrive at conclusions which in the meantime others might have reached before him – 'which is to say,' he went on, 'that in effect I would never have got there at all – because once such discoveries are made they cannot be made a second time.' And in a note specifically on his Nobel Prize (it may have been the text of an acceptance speech) he wrote, 'I accept this prize humbly, on behalf of my team and my university, and most particularly I accept it on behalf of the late Dr Claudia Strange. Her work as much as my own earned this reward.'

But the more Jack Gibbs acknowledged her share in his success the more the acknowledgement was taken as proof of a debt amounting to theft, and at the same time as a cover-up of its real extent. At best it was seen by Claudia's advocates as an admission of guilt, at worst as a forestalling of his critics – dust thrown in their eyes. It was said that he had made use of her during those first years of marriage and then, once his great breakthrough had been made, had simply abandoned her in favour of another woman – one who was no use to him as a scientist, but who would be compliant and easy-going at home.

These decades of feminism have not been fortunate for a man in his position. Jack Gibbs has his glory – his professorial chair, his Nobel Prize, his knighthood – but over it all has fallen the terrible shadow of the Wronged Woman. It is the shadow of Claudia Strange.

Jack appeared in Claudia's life soon after our return from Paris and at a time when I was sure we were about to become lovers. From that moment on everything changed between us. There were fewer letters. She did not any longer even take the trouble to torment me. If she gave me pain it was only by

143

accident. We met seldom now, and since it was always at my suggestion, never hers, I could hardly complain that I had to listen to monologues about her new supervisor (she had contrived to put herself into Jack's charge almost at once), her new lover (that followed as the night the day), the new star in her heavens, the new principle governing her universe . . .

I exaggerate, do I? Only a little, if at all. Of course I was hurt to see myself fading from her consciousness, like the thin, frail wisp of a vanishing comet. But I don't misrepresent her mood of that time. She seemed inspired, a muse of the laboratory, a poet of mathematical calculus; and so totally focused on Jack and on his work it doesn't surprise me that in time he would come to feel it was her thinking as much as his own that carried him over the final obstacles.

She invited me to their wedding in Cambridge, and I think five years must have passed after that (for me) painful occasion before I heard anything more than the most commonplace scraps of news about them – that they were in America; that they were working together, making important discoveries; that they had one child – and so on.

Then they returned to Cambridge and the news became harder, and darker. Soon it was generally known that their marriage was on the rocks and they had separated. Claudia had custody of their little son, Michael, but Jack, who was now living with another woman, took him two or three times a week when Claudia came to London where she had her own small flat and a part-time teaching post in one of the Colleges of London University.

I heard all of this from former Cambridge friends, and I remember noticing that whenever her name was mentioned there was a moment when I felt as if I were short of breath. I did nothing. But I waited in hope and fear – hope that she might get in touch with me, fear of how it would affect me if she did. Finally there was a meeting, just one, at which nothing happened, and everything happened, and soon afterwards she was dead.

The biographies trace in detail her final two weeks of life during a vacation when she could choose to be either in Cambridge or in London. They describe how she became depressed, couldn't stand her London flat, moved in with this friend, then that friend; how she went back to Cambridge to be with little Michael, but two days later returned him to his father and came down to London again. They quote her friends' descriptions of her – distraught, confused, rambling (and sometimes ranting) about Jack's infidelity; taking pills by the handful to make herself sleep and then, on waking, more pills to combat her depression.

The last few days are accounted for almost hour by hour; but there is a brief hiatus which the biographers have not been able to fill. One day Claudia made a phone call from a friend's house, after which she seemed cheerful. She dressed carefully in what the friend called 'a nice dress', did her hair, put on makeup, and vanished for most of the afternoon. When she returned she was silent, shut in on herself. She gathered up her things saying she was returning to Cambridge, but that is not where she went. Next morning she was found dead in her Paddington flat.

I have never visited Claudia's grave and I'm told it's difficult to find because the gravestone, which had become the object of feminist attacks, was long ago removed. Jack's name on the original inscription had been scored over, spray-painted, obscenely maligned. He was a rapist, a thief of intellectual property, a wife-murderer. I met him once in the late 1970s when this onslaught was at its height and getting maximum publicity in the newspapers. He was bitter, of course; but more than anything, he was bewildered. He said the grave would be put right one of these days, but it might have to wait a long time.

Jack, some have said, has been too polite to speak in his own defence – the perfect gentleman. That is partly true, I suppose, but I wonder whether he has really had any choice. To defend himself would have involved saying things against Claudia, complaining about her extravagances and outrages (the occasion, for example, when she burned some of his most important research notes), and that would have been, in effect, to conduct their private quarrels over again in the public arena at a time when she could not speak for herself. It would have been said that he wished to deny her her posthumous fame (which of course he did not), and would only have put further weapons into the hands of his enemies. He would not have been able to deny that, while Claudia had loved him passionately and faithfully, he had left her for another woman. And as for his being a scientist who had used, and profited by, his wife's intellectual brilliance, that was a matter for which he had himself frankly provided the evidence.

So while her case has been made by others, ever more extravagantly (and they are extravagances for which Claudia cannot be blamed, and which she would certainly have deplored), Jack, almost of necessity, has held his tongue.

The call I had hoped for and dreaded came at one of those wonderful winter moments when the day, for hours unrelentingly grey, had all at once begun to release a brilliant shower of snow. One wants to say that things are like other things – a sky like lead, or pewter, and the snow falling out of it like confetti, or the petals of white roses. But if you grew up, as I did, in a place where snow never falls, then perhaps you recognise more clearly its uniqueness. That kind of sky is like nothing but itself; and snow falls only like the falling of snow. For the phone to ring at just that moment, for the voice to be the only one that had always caused a momentary shortness of breath – these were circumstances that seemed to promise to a thirty-year-old academic, weary of London and faintly home-sick, new life, adventure, escape.

She said, in her imperious way, that she wanted to visit me at home – now, at once – and though the prospect made me nervous I said of course she must come. I have a vivid memory of our conversation, she sitting on the floor on an Indian rug with her knees up, I on the edge of the bed which took up a good share of my small living space. It was hardly a conversation at all, more a monologue – a catalogue of woes and wrongs, to which I contributed appropriate exclamations of surprise and sympathy. She talked incessantly about the woman – 'the blonde moron bitch' – for whom Jack had left her. Claudia was, she assured me, 'burning in the hell of jealousy.'

'I feel it,' she went on (and she grasped her crotch with both hands) '*here.*'

There was no doubt what she wanted, and it would be a feeble euphemism to say she wanted me to make love to her. She wanted me to fuck her; and not for her pleasure, nor for mine. At that moment I did not exist, except as an instrument of revenge against Jack Gibbs whom she had loved with an all-consuming passion and who had betrayed her.

It would perhaps earn me a few poor marks for good conduct if I wrote now that I was too high minded to let her engage in an act which, when it was over, would have left her no happier, no nearer a solution to her problem. But when I try to think clearly about what must have been my own inner processes, I know that that thought, though a part of what determined the outcome, was only a very small part, certainly not the deciding one. In fact I think the recognition of how her single-mindedness had expunged me as anything but a weapon against Jack might have released me into action. In the simple physical sense I had always wanted her, and still wanted her. Why then, if at last she had a use for me, should I not have a use for her? That thought was certainly present to me, and would have been uppermost but for something else – a small practical impediment.

It was something so trivial, so much a matter of chance, it belongs only to the category of the absurd. The snow which had so brilliantly showered down just before her phone call had stopped, and there was even a slight break in what had been the unrelenting grey of the sky. Not full sunlight, but new light, was on Claudia's head, and the glint of it in her brown hair reminded me that the heavy curtains, and the gauze ones which protected my domestic interior from eyes in the windows directly across the lane, had just that morning been removed by my landlady. They were to be dry-cleaned and would be returned, she promised, before nightfall.

So mixed with, even dominating, what might be presented as a profound moral dilemma, an occasion of high drama, one of the determining moments in the final days and hours of a woman who has become, and deservedly, something of a modern hero, there was a calculation going on, unspoken and never finally resolved, in the head of a person who was then, and is now, of no importance in Claudia's story. I was like the torturer's horse in the poem by W. H. Auden, scratching its innocent backside against a tree while the dreadful martyrdom runs its course. Could we, I was asking myself, make love – could we *fuck* – on that bed, in full view of the maisonette just across the lane, where the woman who took such an interest in everything beyond her windows was working at her kitchen bench? In the 1990s the answer might have been yes; but this was 1963, and I was not only 'skinny' – I was shy.

Claudia read my hesitation as unwillingness, my silence as cowardice – a fear of saying no – and her response was predictable. There was in those days (has it really changed?) a rule, or perhaps not so much a rule as an unavoidable truth in human relationships, that in such encounters, where there was an invitation to sex, a woman might say no and give no offence – indeed the refusal was often expected; but a man to whom a woman offered herself was almost obliged to accept. To say no to one who had so generously and courageously put herself beyond the pale of propriety would be deeply insulting.

Claudia's anger was huge, though it didn't express itself in shouting or breaking things. It simply expanded like a cloud, the black genie emerging from the bottle of her wrath – so dark, so pungent, so negative, that if some solution to the problem of the missing curtains had at that moment occurred to me, it would have been too late.

As she got up to go her silence was saying, 'I needed you and you failed me' – and it was true. That silence has gone on saying it ever since. She did not need the particular person who answered to my name, but she needed significant action as a release from her torment. She needed a sense that she had some power left – that she could hit back at Jack, and that she had done it. What would it have mattered whether it was wise action or foolish? What would it have mattered if the woman across the street had seen us, or if I, troubled by all these circumstances, had proved a less than wonderful lover? Something should have happened – anything – to fill her mind, to make her feel some relief from the accumulated pain Jack's desertion had given her, and from the depression it had caused.

I have thought about her often in the intervening three decades, and what strikes me always are the multiple ironies: that the woman who demanded brawn, and died for love of a man, should have become a hero of radical feminism; that the man who made the world aware of her genius should be represented as the thief of her fame; that a woman so turbulent should have been such a cool and brilliant analyst of scientific data; that someone who said her life was ruled by fear of death should have killed herself; that the survivor, Jack, should be silenced by the death which has given her a public voice; even (and this is not something I can believe, or want to believe, but which hovers there like dark laughter) that I, who had neither power nor influence in her life, might have saved it if only my landlady had not removed my curtains.

It is not just traditional literature that asks for heroes and villains. Ideology clamours for them even more, while perhaps reality, if we can only see it clearly, permits of neither. That evening, after her visit to my bedsit, Claudia went back to her friends' house, then to her flat in Paddington where she ate a meal, wrote several messages and postcards, including the last of the long and brilliant letters to her sister which have since been published, and went out to post them. She drank some whisky and water, took a handful of her sleeping pills, went to bed with her little handgun under her pillow; and then, perhaps waking later in the night, or possibly as she was drifting asleep, she shot herself in the head.

There was little publicity about her death, and since my relationship with her was hardly known (she liked to keep her life in discrete compartments) no one told me of it. So two days after her visit when I received a card from her, I took it to be a sort of olive branch – mocking, but also forgiving. I was just then on the brink of a visit to the United States, so I took off thinking that perhaps when I returned we might re-establish our friendship. This time, I resolved, I would do better. I would behave more like a man of substance; a man who might be (as the New Life Superstore's machine so recently put it) 'light' in frame, but one who had bulk of *character*.

I still have the postcard, of course, along with my other few mementoes of Claudia. It reads,

C.–
One weepy tramp went for a wimp. He escaped.
No regrets,

      – C.

It is a long time ago, and all that is left composes itself now as in a marble frieze. Claudia shines – she has her glory in death. Jack is there – he has life, and his tarnished fame. Those who played a part in the tragedy, loving or hating, helping or failing to help – they all have their places in the picture. And right at the edge, already turning away, there is the insignificant fellow who was once made anxious by an absence of curtains. He has his anonymity – and his story.

A Short History of New Zealand

HE WAS 52 AND HAD THAT LONDON LOOK – DRY HAIR (he ran his fingers through it, glancing at himself in the lift mirror), tired eyes, something unhealthy about the skin; the suggestion of less than perfect cleanliness, which, like Lady MacBeth's 'damned spot', no amount of washing would quite remove. Was there a word for it? 'Care-worn' sounded too Victorian and virtuous. 'Stressed' was its modern and equally self-serving equivalent.

Within himself he felt little of this – only allowed the recognition to run through his mind, thinking it was how she, a 26-year-old fresh from New Zealand, would see him. As the lift doors opened he caught sight of her sitting in Reception. It was her knees that registered first, primly side by side, in dark stockings, with neat knee-caps and a fine curve away from each side, cut off by the line of the skirt. Good strong Kiwi legs, he thought; and then remembered how when he'd first come to England it had seemed to him that young Englishwomen had no calf muscles. It wasn't true any longer. In the intervening decades Europe had become athletic.

She looked in his direction and must have guessed he was the man she was to meet, but he went first to the desk and said he would be out until three.

'James Barrett,' he said taking the hand she held out to him. 'And you're Angela McIlroy.'

Out in the street she'd lost her bearings. He pointed down Farringdon Street to where the figure of Justice over the Old Bailey lifted sword and scales against the dome of St Paul's. The sun glared down through the haze, casting no decisive shadows. The thump of a 24-hour disco came up through a basement grating. Believing he knew how dingy and confusing these streets must seem to her, he hailed a taxi and gave directions.

They were settled at a table under a tree in a pub yard near the British Museum and had made their choices before he took the little tape machine from his pocket and propped it between the pepper and salt.

'You won't mind, will you?' he asked, and she shook her head. She was unassertive, making no attempt to impress him. Shy, he decided; slightly apprehensive, but self-contained – and he made a mental note of these descriptions.

No need to turn on the machine yet; no need to begin at once with her novel, which was the purpose of the interview. Better to begin – where else? – at their common beginning. She knew he'd grown up in New Zealand? – left as a young man intending to return, but had married an Englishwoman and . . .

Yes, she knew all that. She'd been told. 'Interesting,' she added, nodding and smiling – but he could see it was something other than interest she felt. Disapproval, perhaps? Or was it just indifference?

'I've been back, of course, but only for short stays – three weeks at most. There were eighteen years I never set foot in the place. By then it was too late.'

She'd ordered a salade niçoise. He watched her struggling to cut the lettuce in its bowl. Her drink was mineral water.

'Quite sure?' he asked, lifting his bottle of Italian white.

She held up one hand, like a policeman. Her mouth was full of salad. He filled his glass.

'Oh dammit,' she said, draining the mineral water and holding out her glass. 'Why not?'

'Why not?' he agreed, filling her glass.

'I'm not abstemious,' she said. 'Not especially. But jet-lag and wine . . .'

He nodded. 'Here's to *A Short History of New Zealand*.'

They touched glasses and drank, but the naming of her novel seemed to bring back that wariness which just for a moment he'd thought was about to be cast aside. She fell silent, waiting for him to lead their conversation.

'I read a large part of it coming down on the train this morning. It's quite a grim picture.'

She inclined her head.

'And a true one, so far as I can judge.' And then, almost without meaning to, he began to talk as the expatriate. Once started, it was hard to stop. Some part of his mind was detached. Was this the way to go about it? But then, why not? Somehow he had to get a response out of her.

His view of New Zealand was almost entirely negative, and at first, from the way she met his eyes, nodded, murmured assent, he could see he was taking her with him. But then he went too far. He felt it himself, and saw it in her eyes. Even New Zealand's weather, it seemed, was now inferior. This was London's third good summer in succession. She put her hand over her mouth, and her eyes were smiling.

He looked down at the tablecloth and thought for a moment. 'I'm a journalist,' he said firmly. 'Sometimes when I get a twinge of the old nostalgia I just let myself think what it would have been like working on the *Herald* or the *Dom* or the *Press*, or the *ODT* for God's sake – just imagine it! – dealing with local cow and sheep stories, while all the world stuff was coming in on the wire, written by someone else.'

She nodded, but with such a blank face he began to feel irritation. Did she want him to write about her book? Did she understand that he was doing her a favour? 'My paper has a million readers,' he said.

Her face softened, as if there was something she understood. 'You've done well,' she said.

Her novel, *A Short History of New Zealand*, began with these sentences:

'One's name is Brent and the other is Hemi. One is white and one brown, and they are running under the moon. Ahead and behind and in all directions stretches away the landscape of the plains. You could say they are the cop and the robber. You could say they are the colonist and the colonised. You could say they are the Pakeha and the Maori.

'They are running through most of a long night. Sometimes they stop for breath. Sometimes Hemi reaches the end of his tether and turns on Brent. Pursuer is pursued, back over the same ground. But then it resumes, the other way. They run and keep running.'

The novel is set in a very small town – what used to be called a settlement – in the North Island. It has one cop, a young man who belongs to the local rugby club and takes long training runs with his team-mates. One night he's taking a last look around when he hears something in a storage shed. He goes looking. There are some tense moments in the silence and darkness of the shed – he's sure someone's there but can't find him – and then the burglar, a Maori, makes a break for it, straight out and down the wide main street, the cop in pursuit. In a couple of minutes they've left the town behind. They're out on the open road, running under the moon through that empty landscape, sometimes on the road, sometimes across ploughed fields, through bush, along stream-beds, back to the road again.

The Pakeha sprints. So does the Maori. They slow to jogging, recovering breath. The Maori sprints and the Pakeha almost loses him – but not for long. Sometimes the pursuit slows to a walk, or stops. They talk back and forth across a safe gap, reason with one another, threaten, shout insults.

Then they run again.

With the Sunday papers tucked under one arm he walked back from the village, over ploughed fields, skirting the wood where pheasants, bred for the annual shoot, scuttled away into the undergrowth. The gamekeeper had set snares for foxes, simple loops of fine wire along the edges of pathways. James tripped them as he went. He liked the sight of foxes appearing on his lawn. Why shouldn't those handsome predators, as well as the tweedy kind for whose sport it was intended, have game for supper?

Anne was waiting for him on the gravel outside the front door. He could see by the way she held her hands, and then by her anxious expression, that something was wrong. There had been a phone call from New Zealand. It was bad news. His mother . . .

He flew non-stop. There was no choice if he was to be there for the funeral. It meant eleven hours in the air to Los Angeles, a stop of two hours, and then on again – another twelve to Auckland. His grief was confused with jet-lag and a dread of finding himself among relatives with whom he believed he could have nothing in common. But after the service, when they'd gathered at his sister's Mt Eden house, drinking and eating and talking on the verandah and out on the back lawn, it came over him how much he was enjoying himself. The hugs of cousins he didn't at first recognise brought surges of old affection. Trivial reminiscences gave him pleasure. It even pleased him to be called Jamie. He'd expected to find himself behaving in a way that would be judged aloof, unfriendly, superior, but it wasn't like that at all. In his strange, jet-lagged state it was as though he saw it all from the outside – saw a different self emerge and take over – warm, outgoing, filial, fraternal, avuncular.

Once or twice in his life a death and funeral had had this effect. He hadn't wept. He'd become an actor on a public stage. But this time it was different – something to do with these people, and with the green of the plum tree in new leaf, and the white of pear-blossom, and the freshness of air and light and water. How long was it since he'd felt such uncomplicated happiness?

He remembered that when he was a boy he would meet his mother unexpectedly in a room or in the garden and they would smile – not anxiously, just with the pleasure each felt at seeing the other. The sadness of that thought didn't spoil his happiness. It was part of it.

Late in the day he was asked the inevitable question: how was he finding New Zealand? It would have been easy to evade – to say it was only hours since he'd stepped off the plane. But what came out was 'great' and 'super' and 'wonderful to be home'. He knew it was the right answer; but it was as if, at least for that moment, it was true.

His questioner smiled, glad to hear it, but then shook his head. 'This country's a mess, Jamie. I don't like to say it, but the fact is *you're better off where you are.*'

That night he crashed asleep while the others were still drinking and talking, then woke in the early hours of the morning. He was in the back room of his sister's house, with wide windows looking out on the garden that was overhung with pongas and cabbage trees. The silence was so complete he strained for something that would prove he hadn't lost his hearing. A floorboard creaked – that was all. These wooden houses shifted with the changes in temperature.

A light shower began to fall, whispering on the iron roof. In childhood rain on the roof had always brought sleep, but now he lay listening, soothed but wide awake, his body still on London time.

He turned on the bedside lamp and looked in his bag for Angela McIlroy's novel, and beside it his tape recorder. He put the machine close to his ear, switched it on, and put out the light.

'The framework of your novel's the chase, but in alternating chapters you go back into the lives of the two men – family history, childhood, schooling . . . Did you feel you could do that equally – I mean with confidence . . .'

'I don't think I felt confident about any of it. I just jumped in and hoped I wouldn't sink.'

'Well, clearly you didn't sink. It's rather unusual, from a woman novelist. Not about . . . Not the usual sub . . .'

'They have mothers and sisters.'

'Yes, but the central characters . . .'

'You don't find them convincing?'

'Oh yes, I think so. Sure. As for the, ah – the Maori background . . . Well, I guess – who knows? I think only a Maori could say.'

'I'm not sure . . . I don't think I agree with that. I mean anyone, Maori or Pakeha, could say they felt it was right. Or they felt it was wrong. If you're talking about feeling, that is. Of course if facts are wrong, that's different. But no one . . .'

'No, I'm not suggesting that.'

There was a break. In the background could be heard the clatter of plates, the murmur of other conversations, a burst of loud laughter.

'Look, I don't know how to put this – I'm just feeling my way towards something. It's certainly not a criticism of your novel which I think is well written and well shaped. But the way it's done touches on something . . .'

'Delicate?'

'Delicate – yes. But I think I mean . . . big. I'm not making myself clear, am I.'

'Keep going.'

'It's there in the title – a short history of New Zealand. That's quite a claim. Quite an indictment.'

'Oh an indictment. Is that what it is?' There was the sound of her laughter. 'I think I plead the fifth.'

It was no longer a matter of law and order, or crime and punishment. It had become a question of who was fitter, stronger, cleverer; who would out-run, or out-fox, the other; who would win.

Those roads are long and straight, and when Brent saw headlights in the far distance he thought here was his chance. He would flag down the driver and tell him to call in help. But even while he was thinking this there was the twanging of fence wire and the Maori was off overland. He got a bit of a break on there, and quite soon, after crossing a couple of paddocks, he was in a field of corn. Something had happened to the crop. It was head-high but it seemed to be dried out, dead on the stalk and unpicked. The Maori plunged into it and disappeared. Brent hunted and then stopped. It was such a still night you couldn't move in there and not be heard. If there'd been a wind the Maori could have moved under cover of the rustling, but there was none. And the moon was bright. So Brent waited and rested. When the Maori made a break for it the chase was on again.

They ran through empty fields, through flocks of sheep, through cow-paddocks, through stubble, through crops of swedes and potatoes and cabbages, always well clear of farm-houses. Dogs barked in the distance. A nightbird sounded as they ran through the edges of a swamp. They came back to a road and ran on it. Then there was again the twanging of fence-wire and they were off over a field of onions. The onions had been turned up by a mechanical digger – they were lying on top of the soil, waiting to be collected, and they made it hard going. The Maori seemed to go over on one. It must have rolled under his foot, his ankle twisted, and for just a moment he went down.

'Now you bastard,' Brent thought. And then he wondered, What the fuck am I going to do with him? How'm I going to bring him in?

When he got to him the Maori was up on one knee, holding a knife. 'Come and get it, Dog-breath,' he said.

On the tape they sounded at first hesitant with one another, wary. He'd known it was because she distrusted him as an expatriate, expected him to be patronising. It had made it hard for him to get to the more difficult, and therefore more interesting, questions. But as the lunch went on, and she shared his wine, the exchanges had become more frank, less hesitant.

He ran the tape forward, and listened again.

'I keep coming back to your title . . .'

'Yes, it's bold, I know.'

'And it makes how the thing ends important.'

'Don't tell me about it. Terribly important. I spent so many months agonising over all that. I kept rewriting the end – it never seemed right. Then I'd give away the title – look for something more modest. But that seemed the easy way out. The cowardly . . . You see I'd had the title in mind right from the start – before I'd written a word. That, and the basic story of the all-night chase, which was something that happened. I read about it in the paper, and straight away I thought this is a short history of New Zealand. But it had such symbolic force – too much. Pakeha chases Maori through his own land to enforce British law. Every now and then Maori rebels and turns on Pakeha, but then it's back to the old chase. That was okay in a way – as a story – because it was real. It happened, and it was believable. But if it was to carry that symbolic load . . .'

'That's why the end . . .'

'Yes, because it's not finished, is it? I mean the history's not. It goes on . . . So the end of the novel has to be – what's the word?'

'Tentative? Not definitive?'

'Yes, that's right, but . . . *Provisional*. That's the word. I had it on a piece of paper pinned over my desk. The ending had to be provisional. The first version ended with an arrest. They ran all night and then early in the morning Hemi just lost heart and gave up. Well, that might be how it would happen – but as symbol . . .'

'No good. I can see that. They haven't given up.'

'And then I had him get away. No good again, you see. Too easy. Sentimental. Because the real history . . .'

'Yes, it's tougher than that.'

'Then I had them fight it out. But how does that end? Pakeha kills Maori? Maori kills Pakeha? They're both killed? They make friends and walk off hand in hand into the sunrise? You see? Nothing seemed to fit.'

'Not as things are right now. But they're all possible, aren't they?'

'You mean in reality.'

'I mean – what do I mean? They're possible ends, most of them, if you think just of the two men. Maybe the problem is there's too much conflict, d'you think? The story sets them too much in opposition. After all, it hasn't always been like that. If you think of our history . . .'

'Our?'

'Yes . . . Oh, I see. You think as an expatriate it's not mine any more.'

And there the tape ran out.

'Come and get it,' the Maori repeated, holding the knife out in front of him. And then suddenly he was up and running, not away this time, but straight at his pursuer. Brent turned and ran.

The sprint didn't last long. They had run too many miles; but when they stopped the Maori must have felt he was on top.

'Okay', he said. 'Just fuck off and I'll let you keep your balls.'

He turned and walked in the opposite direction. It can't have been long before he heard footsteps coming after him, keeping a safe distance. Brent wasn't going to give up now. If he couldn't arrest the bugger, he'd stick with him until daylight.

It took a few runs this way and that before the new rules were established. When the Maori chased, Brent ran. Once it was so close he felt his shirt slashed, and a strange sensation – not pain, a sort of coldness – down his back. He didn't think the knife had cut him, but later he felt a trickle of blood. After that he kept his distance; but as the Maori turned and headed off, he followed.

Now the Maori ran again, effortlessly, as if he was doing it to suit himself. He didn't look back. They came to a stop-bank – it loomed up high and straight above the plain on one side and the river on the other, with a flat grassy path along the top. They went up on to it and kept running, heading down-river towards the sea.

After half an hour they ran off the stop-bank and down a road, and there, opening out in front of them, was the coast – dunes and sand all scattered over with huge white logs and driftwood that had come down the river over the years and gone out to sea only to be washed back by the westerlies. Under the moon it looked like a huge boneyard, with the sea thundering against it.

The Maori seemed to know where he was going now. He stopped short of the dunes and headed north over fields until he came to another road. It was there he went into a pine grove. Brent lost him briefly, and for the first time thought he should give up. He was now a long way from home, and nobody would know where. He might be ambushed and knifed. You could bury a body in the piles of needles and it might not be found for years.

But he kept going, relying on his ears and on the stillness of the night. He stood with his back against a pine trunk and listened. When the Maori moved, Brent went after him.

They came to a clearing and stopped. They were on either side of it, the moon coming through so they could see one another. They rested, sizing one another up. After a while the Maori said, 'You got a wife and kids?'

Brent told him he had a wife, no kids yet.

The Maori turned the knife-blade this way and that on his palm, as if his hand were a razor strop.

'What about you,' Brent asked.

The Maori said, 'Soon I'll introduce you to my mates. They're Rastas.'

Brent didn't reply.

'Where I'm taking you,' the Maori said, 'we got a big hole in the ground, like a cave, eh. We call it a tomo. You ever seen a tomo, Dog-breath? They drop the dead calves down there. Sometimes a whole cow. Not even the stink comes up.'

He turned, out of the clearing, and began walking through the pines. He came to a fence and climbed over it. Over his shoulder he called, 'Come on Pakeha. Let's get there before the sun comes up.'

She'd solved her problem by adding a second layer – the story of the writer writing the story. It was what James had liked least about her novel, but he could see why she'd done it.

There could be no end, so there had to be many ends – many possibilities, all left open. It was called 'meta-fiction' these days and it was very fashionable, but how could you get around the basic human appetite that every story should have a beginning a middle and an end, and that to be enjoyed it had to be believed?

The rain was getting heavier. The whisper on the roof became a rustling, and briefly a roar. There was the sound of water rushing along gutterings and through down-spouts, and dripping from ponga fronds on to the lawn. Then it died away again to a gentle hissing.

He thought of his Northamptonshire garden, the roses and hollyhocks, the woods across fields with crows circling and crying. At last drowsiness returned, and sleep.

He dreamed that he was talking to Angela McIlroy over lunch, or rather, listening while she talked. She spoke in fluent Maori, though words like salade niçoise and frascati were mixed up in it. Now and then she paused in her monologue to turn the blade of her knife back and forth across her open palm.

He strained to catch what it was she was telling him, certain that he did understand – that he was capable of it – but never quite making sense of it. It was like something just beyond reach, or a word on the tip of the tongue.

Brightness Falls from the Air

❦

THE SNOW HAS COME BACK. HENRY KNEW IT THIS morning before getting up and looking out – 'sensed' it; which means, he supposes, that his waking eyes registered the different light, its whiteness.

And Albie has gone again. That too Henry knew while he lay there, because the silence that comes with the other-worldly light of the fallen snow was undisturbed by the poet's frantic work at the typewriter in the next room.

Now, looking out through a window, Henry is watching a cat making its way through the snow, which comes up to its shoulders. It tries a high-stepping walk; then an intermittent leaping. Henry isn't sure what it's looking for, but he supposes food. It stops to shake itself, disliking the sense that its fur is becoming wet, uncertain now whether to go forward or back.

He wonders why the sight of animals going about their daily business gives such pleasure, and decides it's because what they do exactly matches, in scale, what they need to do, whereas our doings are always an excess. He imagines them taking over when we, the human race, become extinct. They must be kin, he thinks, or there would be no pleasure in that thought.

During the past couple of days, while Albie bashed away at

his typewriter and raced in and out to the kitchen and to the bench press on the cold front porch, Henry has observed the squirrels. There was no sign of snow then, and they darted about the campus lawns digging for buried nuts. Though the cold out there was intense even in the sun, it was as if spring must be just around the corner. But yesterday, while the sky was blue and the sun continued to shine, the squirrels' demeanour changed. They knew something Henry didn't know. They were anxious, and not for food. They hung upside down on the boughs and trunks of trees, stripping bark and running up to repair their nests. This morning they're gone, hiding away in those newly patched interiors, and all down the Jersey Shore the snow is falling.

There is no sky, just a low grey blankness out of which the flakes sail like an invasion of paratroopers; and the brightness seems to come, not down from above, but up from below. Light has taken on substantial form. It has broken up and is tumbling out of the heavens. Still shining, it covers lawns and paths; heaps up on hedges, statues, fences, gates; on outdoor chairs and tables. It piles up along branches, and falls from them in sudden, splintering showers. Soon the ploughs will be out to clear the road, and the shovels will attack paths and sidewalks. But for now it comes thick and fast and lies undisturbed.

Henry – Professor Henry Bulov – turns on Woodlake's 'Memory Station' which plays 'the greatest music of all time', by which is meant the popular songs of the 1940s, '50s and '60s. He begins to make breakfast and then, feeling the need of company, changes his mind, puts on overcoat, scarf, gloves, hat, and walks to the campus dining room where the nuns will smile and urge him to eat more, to keep warm, to look after himself.

That over, he will wait for the ploughs and shovels to do their work before walking the mile or so to the supermarket.

There's nothing he needs there, but it's somewhere to go. Meanwhile, there is the latest batch of poems Albie has given him to read – more of the same he has read and re-read this past fortnight. By now Henry knows what to expect. They will be sharp, pictorial, 'Japanesy', occasionally witty, now and then gritty. But where has the grand sweep gone, the larger scale? Where are the Modernist ambulations, the parodic dislocations of the post-Modern? What has become of the great Canadian epic-maker and courage-teacher, delineator of northern wastes, servant of the mythical White Queen, poet-father of the Snow Maiden? Where among all these miniaturist nail-parings is the majesty that was Alban Ashtree?

Crunching through the dry snow, up to his ankles in it, Henry says over to himself lines from a 17th century poet whose name eludes him, and wonders whether they have sprung to mind because of the snow or because of the decline of a once major poet:

> *Brightness falls from the air,*
> *Queens have died young and fair,*
> *Lord, have mercy upon us.*

But this is a story, and we must go back two weeks to take up the thread.

Henry Bulov, recently appointed full professor by his university in New Zealand, arrived at JFK with his modest and battered baggage and was met at the foot of the escalator below the American Airlines desk by a Gofar Limo driver holding up a sign with a version of his name he hadn't encountered before:

PROF BELOVE

He shook hands with the driver and they joked about the mistake. Henry told him about the fax from Woodlake

College saying he would be met by a representative of the Gofar Limp Company.

There was a sixty mile drive south to Woodlake. Henry sat in the back and pretended to read papers, pretended to sleep, did sleep – but not before he had had his views of the Manhattan skyline across water in the fading light, and seen the Staten Island 'hills' that were really New York's garbage mountains. When he woke it was dark and they were somewhere in the State of New Jersey, pulling in at the doors of a restaurant built out over a river or tidal inlet.

Ashtree, known now as Albie Strong, met him at the door. It was their first encounter, and the greetings were loud and enthusiastic, the smiles broad, the handshakes strong.

'We're dining alone,' Albie explained. 'There are things I have to get straight with you.'

There were indeed. The circumstances of Henry's invitation had been mysterious – not surprisingly since it was generally understood that the poet Alban Ashtree was dead, killed (though the body had never been recovered) in an avalanche in the Austrian Alps. It was a death which had always given Henry anxiety. It lacked the sense of perfect closure that ought to accompany a genuine demise. There was an air of fiction, even of contrivance, about it. It had been too good to be true – iconologically apt (Ashtree was poet and theorist of the Snow-White Goddess), and lexically perfect, the author's name piling up in alliteration with place and event. 'Alban Ashtree,' Henry's book on him began, 'died in an avalanche in the Austrian Alps.' It had been the easiest sentence to write and the hardest to believe. Even the Canada Council, afflicted by doubts, had frozen the funds set aside for the posthumous editing of Ashtree's work.

But this uncertainty had only added to the aura surrounding Ashtree's name and his poetry. The man for so long known only in his own country was soon being talked about in New York and in London. Two years after his 'death' the work, previously published only in Canada, was available everywhere in English, and translations into several European languages were appearing or planned. And Henry Bulov, the first non-Canadian to write seriously about Ashtree, and the only person (no one knew how this had come about) to have read his private notebooks, had found the academic escalator, for so long stalled beneath his feet, all at once lurching on up to full professorial status. Bulov had helped to make Ashtree famous; Ashtree's fame had helped to make Bulov respectable. These two, it seemed, needed one another; and now, improbably ('It's like a story,' Henry said, as they gave up the handshaking and embraced one another) here they were meeting for dinner in a New Jersey restaurant that looked out over moonlit waters.

Albie (as he asked to be called) was a tall, well-constructed fifty-two-year-old with a good head of grey hair tied back in a pony-tail. He wore jeans, boots, a shirt of red corduroy, and a leather jacket. He talked fast, ate fast, seemed impatient, but also excited to be meeting the critic who had done so much to promote his work and his reputation.

The Austrian avalanche, he told Henry, had been real. He had been taken up by it, swept down the mountain slope, and then, by some miracle, or quirk of the rolling snow, had been ejected – cast out on to a ridge from which he had been able to make his way down to a village on the lower slopes. He was bewildered, slightly concussed, and it was some hours before he recovered his sense of who and where he was. By that time the news was everywhere. Seven were missing, four already confirmed dead.

With the least possible fuss he returned to his ski lodge, where he had gone unaccompanied, removed a few essentials, and departed, leaving gear by which he could be identified. Next day, from a village further down the mountain he rang two newspapers, one in Toronto, the other in Vancouver, to report the death of the poet Alban Ashtree. It was meant only to bring him a little attention, but the story ran all across Canada, from east to west, from west to east, its authenticity never seeming to be checked. Though for a time he travelled on his own passport, and drew on his own bank account, no one appeared to notice. As far as the Canadian literary and academic community were concerned the fact was established: Alban Ashtree the poet had died in that avalanche.

During what remained of his sabbatical year Ashtree's fame spread, promoted especially by an article Henry Bulov wrote for the *Times Literary Supplement*. Unused to his work receiving the kind of attention he always believed it deserved, Albie now found the condition of being dead difficult to give up. Casually at first, and then, as time passed, purposefully, he contrived a new life for himself, one which allowed him to keep his death alive. This involved difficulties and sacrifices. Posing as a former anti-Vietnam defector-to-Canada whose previous identity had to remain undisclosed, he had been able to get a teaching post in a minor, though well-endowed, Catholic college. But he was not able to profit by, or to enjoy (except as an observer), Alban Ashtree's increasing fame. Part of him wanted to reclaim it as his own; a more cautious self recognised that to 'come back' might be to lose it.

'I'm like the lover on the Grecian urn,' he told Henry. 'He lives for ever because he's a work of art. But because he's a work of art he's not flesh and blood – he can't kiss the girl.'

But was he intending to stay dead for ever? – that was what Henry needed to know. He put the question in a way which sounded odd even as he said it: 'Will you ever come back to life?'

Ashtree smiled. 'It's a hard one, Henry. If I do, there's going to be hell to pay. A massive critical backlash, wouldn't you say? That's why there have to be new poems first, and they have to be good.'

What he impressed on Henry during that first meeting was that in the meantime his real identity must remain secret. It was not known to anyone – not to Woodlake College which employed him; not even to the woman in his life, Joy Gates, also a teacher at the college. During the past few years Albie Strong had acquired a modest reputation as a poet of the Jersey Shore. Woodlake College had issued two small collections of his new work. He gave readings, poetry workshops, was interviewed on local radio and written about in the local papers.

'No one connects my work with Ashtree's,' he explained. 'The new stuff is different. Smaller in scale.' There was a look of uncertainty as he said this. 'Tighter. Closer to the knuckle.'

After a short silence, which Henry couldn't think how to plug, Albie murmured, 'Hopefully.'

Henry was to share Albie's house on the edge of the campus. He was to read the new work, comment on it, prepare for a time when it might seem right to reveal that the two poets, Alban Ashtree and Albie Strong were one; but he was to say nothing until Albie gave the word, which might be soon or might be years away. It was possible even that it might have to wait until he died – in which case Henry would be named as his literary executor. This was something they would discuss. Together they would arrive at a strategy.

'I need someone to tell me how I'm going with my work,' Albie said when the meal was eaten and they were sitting over their decafs. 'You're the critic I can trust, Henry. The only one.' Again there was that uncertain look, but also a glimmer of courage. 'You have to give it to me straight, man.'

In the days since that first meeting Henry has begun to understand why Albie's confidence is less than perfect. With his real name and nation has gone, it seems, his real strength as a poet. Away from Canada and the northern wastes that were his inspiration, Alban Ashtree's talent has shrivelled. As poet of the Jersey Shore, he is Samson after the haircut. What remains of his former strength is a sort of sad afterglow.

So the visit, embarked on with such enthusiasm, has turned into a trial of character for Henry. Should he be truthful, and if so when? When a poet says, 'You have to give it to me straight, man,' is he to be taken at his word? Even if he means it, that's not to say he won't react badly when he gets it. And wouldn't the truth be like a death sentence? It would be saying in effect, 'Don't come back to life if you want Alban Ashtree's reputation to continue.'

But there are more immediate problems for Henry. Albie is not easy to share a house with. More precisely, Albie is extremely difficult to share anything with. All day, when he's not teaching, he sits at a desk in his room, hammering away at an old-fashioned typewriter in furious bursts interspersed with long silences and occasional eruptions of swearing, or singing, or muttering, or laughing – the latter a kind of dark laughter, more sinister than the swearing and muttering. Albie, Henry writes in the journal he is keeping, is a sort of Glenn Gould of the lexical keyboard.

At intervals of about half an hour the poet jumps from his chair and rushes either to the front porch or to the kitchen. On the porch he has set up his bench press and weights. The lifting is accompanied by huge orgasmic groans and sighs. When the rush is to the kitchen he fills a bowl with fat-free granola and a fat-free fruit-yoghurt drink, downs it at speed, and returns to his room and his desk. There are no regular meals, but if Henry wants them he can take them at the university dining room.

'This is better than my old regimen,' Albie explains, leaning against the door-jamb of Henry's room while he spoons out the last of a bowlful. 'Before Joy I only used to eat every second day. The starvation days were hell. You wouldn't have liked living with me then.'

Albie works till late, then unfolds an ironing board and stands at it while he watches a replay of the old *Star Trek* series. He irons not only shirts and handkerchiefs, but underclothes, sheets, pillow-cases, towels – everything. When there's nothing left, he re-irons clothes already done. The ironing, Henry has come to realise, is only because Albie needs something to do, can't sit still while watching.

Then he takes sleeping pills, puts a rolled towel across his bedroom door, and turns on what he calls 'radio static', a sort of white noise, to drown out all external sound. When Henry gets up in the night to go to the bathroom he hears that strange loud continuous hissing coming from Albie's bedroom.

Fortunately Albie is not there all the time. There are days and nights when, as now, he is at Joy Gates's house, twenty miles away in a town called Brick. Then Henry has only to cope with the loneliness of the little suburban house at the edge of the campus, a house in which the furnishings and pictures provided by the nuns, sober, dull, proper, self-abnegating (and including by way of uplift only a golden Christ on a midnight-blue cross over the living room door) fight a Cold War with the items Albie has introduced – a Tiffany lampshade over an art deco dining table in black glass on a red central column; a shiny red plastic wall-hanging representing an English telephone box; an Algonquian shield and spear; several big-faced 1940s electric clocks advertising dairy products, motor oil, piston rings; a white sofa with red cushions; a telephone in transparent plastic which lights up in blue when it rings; a print from the Utamaro brothel series. Slowly the sensibility of Albie is winning its interior décor war against the pale restraining hands of the Sisters of Mercy, but there are battles yet to be fought and in the meantime no truce is in prospect. The Joseph House, as it is called, is not a house of peace.

Henry leaves it to walk to the supermarket. By now the ploughs have done their work on the roads, and the pavements are partly cleared, but patches of ice make the going on foot slow and dangerous. Up and down the street men are out with shovels. Without exception they are dressed in black with broad-brimmed hats, some with a long lock of hair trailing somewhere over face or neck. These are Hasidic Jews, and the suburb is full of them. Their wives wear wigs so their hair will not be seen by strangers, their children are innumerable, their cars are large old station-wagons with many dents, and their lawns are covered with plastic toys in bright colours sticking up like wreckage through the whiteness of the snow. The Hasidim are devoted to prayer and propagation, but also (Albie's Random House Dictionary informs Henry) to joy. Their responses to his morning greetings, however, are mostly grim and formal.

It is almost two miles to the shops – far enough for Henry's ears to feel the cold painfully. He buys fruit and cheese and chocolate and wine. At the liquor store he checks his ticket in the New Jersey lottery. He has not won a prize; but the storekeeper tells him there is a huge jackpot coming.

By now the ears have thawed and he is ready for the long march back.

Joy Gates, the woman in Albie's life, is a glamorous, energetic divorcée, a woman in her forties who wins Henry's approval not by cleverness (though she may well be clever, and probably is) nor by charm (though he's quite sure she could charm if she chose), but simply by smiling. Joy's smile is warm, wry, and self-sufficient. It seems to come from good health, acceptance, and an inner electrical charge. No doubt, Henry reflects, it could be defeated, but the circumstances would have to be dire – flood, famine or slaughter.

Joy seems, in her egocentric way, to love her poet and to do all she can to promote his work. She doesn't live with him, however, except overnight, or sometimes for two nights on end, and Henry understands why. No one, not even Joy Gates, could live for long with Albie and keep smiling.

Today, a Saturday, is Joy's mother's seventy fifth birthday, and they are to take her to New York to see a matinee performance of a play by Edward Albee, *Three Tall Women*. Joy has ordered a white stretch limo as part of the birthday treat, and it arrives at the Joseph House a few minutes early. Joy's mother, Gay, is already in the car. They will drive next to the town of Brick to pick up Joy and Albie, and then on up to New York. The driver is wearing a suit and bow-tie. 'Do you have boots, sir?' he asks at the door.

Henry says he doesn't need them.

The driver frowns, looking at the path deep in snow. 'I'll try to clear some of this while you're getting ready, sir.'

Henry tells him not to be silly. 'Wait in the car and keep warm.' But when he emerges the driver is waiting on the porch with a golf umbrella. His eagerness, and the size and whiteness of the stretch, which seems at one moment to vanish into the snow, at another to be materialising out of it, signal generous expense. This is something grander than the Gofar Limo Company. Joy is turning it on for her aged parent.

Inside the limo there are two pairs of leather chairs, facing one another. There is a drinks cabinet, and ice. Gay, in furs and a fur hat, has a face that must once have been pure Hollywood and is still glamorous. She introduces herself, they shake hands and he wishes her a happy birthday.

'Happy birthday?' she repeats, puzzled. And then, 'Oh yes. Sure.' She laughs, revealing a perfect bow of upper teeth, all her own.

It is Saturday and the Jews are walking to the synagogue in family clusters, not along the sidewalks, but in the middle of the suburban street where the snow ploughs have made the deepest impression. The men have shed their broad-brims and are wearing immense fur hats out of Russia or central Europe. The limo crawls behind them. When it tries to go around them there are angry shouts and gestures of protest.

When they get out of the Hasidic suburb and on to the highway Gay begins to tell stories about Joy's infancy. 'She didn't creep like other children. At eight months she just got up and walked. Her first words were, "I do it."'

'"I *do* it"?'

'"*I* do it",' Gay says, putting the emphasis in the right place. 'She was always very independent.'

Yes. Henry can imagine that.

'From the time she was seven,' Gay goes on, 'I never had to manage money. Joy looked after it. When we went shopping, she had the purse. If I bought something, she paid. If I wanted something too expensive she told me I couldn't have it – there wasn't enough in the purse.'

'From the age of seven,' Henry repeats, not disbelieving, but by way of showing that though his eyes are on the woods and the river and the white, transformed landscape, he is listening.

He is aware that Gay must be a widow. He asks about her husband. 'He was a Sioux,' she tells him. 'A beautiful man with a fine body. He was a pilot.'

'So Joy's father was an Indian . . .' He corrects himself. 'A Native American . . .'

But Gay is shaking her head. 'Joy's father was Samuel. Walter was the Sioux.'

'He was your second husband?'

'My third,' she replies, and then appears uncertain. In any case Henry is not sure whether they are now talking about Samuel or Walter.

'What did he – Joy's father – *do*, so to speak.'

Gay's eyes have gone dreamy with reminiscence. 'He was a beautiful man, a pilot, and I lost him . . .'

But wasn't it the Sioux who was the pilot? He gives it up. 'I've heard good things about this play,' he says.

She sighs, still sad at the thought of Walter. 'Is there an orange juice in there?' She is pointing to the drinks cabinet. He opens it and finds what she wants, a bottle, up to its neck in ice. 'I won't have it now,' she says. 'Later.'

He pushes it back into the ice. 'Drinks can make you think you need to eat,' Gay says. 'I eat only once a day, in the morning, and it's all I need. It's how I kept slim. Of course,' she acknowledges, 'I'm not so slim now . . .'

She is not slim, it's true, and he lets this invitation to contradict her pass. There is a long thoughtful silence. Snow has begun to drift down again, and now she is telling him what she cooks for that one meal. There are many items, and she explains in what special way each of them is nutritious.

He stops listening. And then, 'Yes,' he hears her say. 'A play. He's a talented boy isn't he?'

Henry wonders how to deal with this. 'I'm sorry,' he says. 'I drifted off for a moment. Who is talented?'

'Albie.'

'Albie, of course. His poetry . . .'

'His poetry. And now his play.'

His play? Has she confused Albie and Edward Albee? To get it clear which of them is confused, Henry asks, 'What did you say Joy's father did for a living?'

'Samuel,' she says, in a tone both firm and dismissive, 'worked for my father. He was an instructor.'

They are driving now into the town of Brick, and she makes him promise he will not let Joy know that she has told him things about her daughter's infancy. Albie and Joy are waiting at the door of Joy's townhouse.

Before they leave Brick Albie gets the driver to stop at a shop that sells tickets in the lottery. There's a jackpot draw coming that's to be worth at least $35 million. They each put in five dollars. That will give them twenty shots at the pick-six. Albie comes back waving the tickets. 'Thirty-five million among four,' he says. 'I make that eight and a half each, with a million over for a party.'

He stuffs them into his billfold.

'I might go on a world cruise,' Gay says. 'I've never been to foreign places.' She stares out at the snow. 'Or maybe Miami.'

'Los Angeles for you, Mom,' Joy says. 'Hollywood. They'll put you straight into a movie. You'll be a star.'

Gay says, 'When I was young that's what everyone told me. "Go to Hollywood," they said. "You've got the looks. You'll be a star."'

'With eight and a half,' Albie says, 'you could be a star without doing the movie. You could just buy yourself a big house in Brentwood . . .'

Gay purrs. 'I'd like that.'

Albie is restless as they drive on. He keeps checking their speed, the distance covered, the time the play is due to start, the state of roads and weather. He takes ice from the drinks cabinet and sucks or chews it, presses it to his wrists and along the back of his neck. As they get nearer to New York Gay becomes excited. It's a long time since she has seen the city, which was once her home. She recognises landmarks – fuel depots, derelict warehouses, refineries, generators, ash heaps, wreckers' yards – greeting them as if they were things of great beauty. When they come out of the tunnel into Manhattan she lowers her window. 'Halloo New York!' she shouts up at the skyscrapers. 'Hi there, New York! Halloo!'

She turns her face to them, at once smiling and tearful. 'Ah, New York,' she says. 'Isn't it great? And Gene Kelly had to go and die on me. That was a man I would have married.'

The Edward Albee play turns out to be about an unpleasant old woman, attended in the first half by a sadistic nurse and an angry lawyer. These are the three women of the title, and they are named in the programme as A, B and C. There is a lot about A's imperfect control of her bodily functions, and at the end of the act she suffers a stroke. In the second half A, B and C represent A's three selves, old, middle-aged, and young. Her sex-life is recounted – a beautiful teenage experience, unappetising marital sex, and a brief violent affair with a groom in her husband's stables. Throughout this half of the play A, the terminal stroke-victim whose earlier selves these three now represent, lies unconscious in a big bed wearing an oxygen mask.

It is hardly a play to celebrate a woman's seventy-fifth birthday and Henry feels such embarrassment at what seems like a bad mistake he finds it difficult to concentrate. During the second half he's relieved to see that Gay has fallen asleep. Joy rolls her eyes at him across her mother seated between them, as if to signify that she too is embarrassed. But as they come out of the theatre Gay seems refreshed and cheerful. 'Did you write that about me?' she asks Albie.

'Write what?' he asks; and then darts forward in the crowd, looking for the white stretch.

'Of course he won't ever admit it,' Gay says in an undertone to Henry.

They get the driver to take them to a famous deli on Broadway where they order a soup of barley and beans, and then pastrami and gherkin sandwiches which are so large they must contain, each of them, a pound of meat. Gay appears to have forgotten that she eats only once a day. Albie jokes with the waitress, who comes from Costa Rica.

'I like your horse-tail,' she tells him, flipping his tied-back hair with her pencil. 'What else you got like a horse?'

'Hey,' he says. 'Will you marry me?'

'I don' marry no one,' she says. 'I was married once and you know what I say? I say marriage sucks.'

'I see a poem here, guys,' Albie tells them. When she returns with their orders he asks her what was the worst thing about her marriage.

'Getting married was the worst,' she says. 'I was fourteen. And best was when I leave him.'

It is already dark as they drive away from Manhattan with their brown bags of unfinished pastrami which give the heated interior of the limo a strange salty aroma.

That night Albie comes back with Henry to the Joseph House. He doesn't work at his typewriter, is restless, seems constantly on the brink of saying something which doesn't get said. He suggests a walk around the campus and Henry, wanting to be agreeable, goes with him, slipping and skating in the dark along the icy paths.

'I used to love this place,' Albie says as they walk under trees and down towards the lake. 'I'd done that thing in Austria – killed myself off. I didn't belong anywhere. Didn't know what I was going to do. The nuns gave me work, didn't ask too many questions, made me feel at home.' The tone in which all this is said seems to put it firmly in the past.

'Joy . . .' Henry offers.

'A wonderful woman.' Albie says that, too, with a kind of retrospective finality.

They stand staring at floodlit statuary above the lake. It belongs to the time when the grounds and buildings were the mansion estate of a rich railroad-owner. There are classical columns and a naked Grecian youth. On the far side of the water the nuns have added a statue of the Virgin. The Virgin and the boy stare at one another across the ice. 'For ever wilt thou love and she be fair,' Albie quotes.

As they head back towards the Joseph House he says, 'It's truth time, Henry.'

Henry feels a nervous tremor. 'Truth time?'

'My new poems.'

'They're good.' He says it too fast, too brightly, conscious that if he meant it sincerely it would have sounded different. Also that Albie will have registered a lack of conviction.

'How good?'

'I think I need time . . .'

'No, you've had time.'

'To assess . . .'

'You're leaving . . . When?'

'Next week.'

'And before that there's . . .'

'Yes, my visit to Princeton.'

'So let's have it, man. How do they compare?'

'Compare?'

'Compare, Henry, for god's sake. With the earlier stuff. With Ashtree.'

'You wrote them, Albie. They're good. What else could they be?'

Albie doesn't press it any further. There's no need. He knows the thumb has gone down on his new work. They walk on in silence. Back at the Joseph House Albie says, 'You were supposed to give it to me straight.'

Henry has gathered himself now. He has been brought all this way, it seems at Albie's expense, or at least at his behest, and he owes it to the poet to give him what he asks for.

'Okay,' he says. 'They're nice publishable poems. Well-turned, sharp observation, some brilliant images. But no, they're not as good. The range is lost, or the punch, or the guts, or something, I don't know what. The life. Something's missing, Albie.'

Albie smiles at him. 'Attaboy,' he says. 'It wasn't so bad, was it?'

Henry doesn't know how to respond. There seems no bitterness. For just a moment, and it's the only time it has happened since they first greeted one another, Albie looks at ease, as if a weight – of doubt maybe, or responsibility – has been lifted. He pats Henry's arm. 'Thanks for that, friend.'

He goes to his room and shuts the door. Henry waits for the sound of the typewriter. Or will it be a gunshot? After a time he hears the hissing of Albie's white-noise machine.

Henry is away for most of a week. He spends three days at the Princeton University library studying books and manuscripts. There are a couple of days in New York, looking at libraries, visiting museums and art galleries. When he gets back to Woodlake he notices changes in the Joseph House. Albie's room, looked at from the passageway, has become more orderly. The clutter of books and papers seems reduced. The old Olivetti is down on the floor, replaced on the desk by a laptop. There is a cardboard box piled high with discarded files.

The bench press and weights are gone from the front porch. In the living room the Algonquian shield and spear are missing from the walls; so are the Utamaro print and the wall-hanging representing a phone box.

'I was getting tired of those things,' Albie says. 'Time for some changes.'

He does no work at his desk, apart from more tidying and clearing of old papers. That night he borrows two video movies and they watch them together. Both are about life in prison. In one the hero is found guilty of a double murder he didn't commit, and locked up for life. Most of the movie takes place in the prison where he spends more than twenty years. It's a bleak story, but at last he escapes, gets right away to start a new life for himself in some idyllic place with a long white beach, blue water and palm trees.

The other, based on a true story from the old San Quentin

days, is much darker. A prisoner, guilty only of stealing five dollars from a Post Office, tries to escape and as a consequence spends three years in solitary confinement, only taken out at intervals to be beaten and tortured by a sadistic prison superintendent. Driven mad by this treatment, he murders the inmate who gave away the escape plan. His defence lawyer reveals the nature of the torture he has undergone and the prisoner is found not guilty. He is returned to San Quentin to serve out his other sentence and three weeks later is found murdered in his cell.

After four remorseless hours of prison life the interior of the Joseph House looks strange to Henry. To Albie too, it seems, because he says, 'Prisons aren't like that any more'; and then he adds, 'They're more like this place, I guess.'

He opens a bottle of whisky and insists on a nightcap. It's not something Henry likes or wants, but he accepts one drink, then a second, to be sociable. He sleeps soundly but wakes some time after 3 am and heads for the bathroom. There is a light on in Albie's room and the door is open. The bed is unmade and the room wildly untidy, as if stirred by a gigantic spoon. The rolled-up towel has been pushed back by the opening of the door. The white-noise machine is issuing its loud hissing static.

Henry tries to think of a rational explanation – that Albie has gone out for a walk, that he has gone to his office, that he has driven over to Joy's house. But the word that springs into his half-asleep brain is 'Escape'. He looks out to the street and sees that Albie's car is still parked there.

Next morning nothing has changed. Henry calls Joy but Albie is not at her house. He is due to give classes but he doesn't turn up for them.

Two days later Henry is ready to leave Woodlake, and there is still no sign of Albie. He has vanished. Everyone is worried.

The nuns are saying prayers for his safety. The police have been notified. There is talk of dragging the lake.

Joy comes to say goodbye. It is early March and a Jewish festival is taking place. All the children in the neighbourhood are in fancy dress. The men wear their usual black suits and hats, but some have put on red noses, funny face-masks, batman cloaks. The women bustle about carrying cakes in boxes and string bags. The big old bent and broken station-wagons go up and down, filled with shouting children. An ambulance decorated with balloons and streamers is driven around the streets broadcasting music.

Henry's bag is packed and he's ready to go. He stands with Joy looking out into the street waiting for the Gofar Limo car that will take him to JFK. Another snowstorm is coming through and he is worried that he will miss his flight.

'But these storms delay the flights too,' Joy tells him. 'They have to plough the runways and de-ice the wings. If you're late, they will be too.' She gives his hand a reassuring squeeze.

'I'm sorry to be leaving you right now,' he says. 'I wish I could be of use.'

She shakes her head. 'He's gone.'

'You don't mean . . .'

'Not dead. Gone. We won't see him again.'

'Did he say . . .'

'No. Nothing. Not a thing. There was no warning. Maybe that's why I feel so sure.'

'He must be mad.'

She looks up and, recognising what he means, smiles and shakes her head. 'If you mean to flatter . . .'

'I mean to praise.'

She pats his arm. 'Well thank you. But I'm not what he needs.'

Henry resists an urge to tell her that Albie Strong is Alban

Ashtree. A few minutes later the car draws up in the street. Snow is falling fast now.

He hugs her and they say goodbye. He has his suitcase halfway across the porch and is handing it to the driver when she asks, from the door, whether Albie checked their lottery tickets. Henry tells her he doesn't know, hasn't given it a thought. 'He didn't tell you?'

'I forgot to ask.'

'Well, I guess we didn't . . .'

She says, 'Mom tells me there were three tickets shared the prize. One was sold in Trenton, one in Newark, and one in Brick.'

'One in Brick.' Henry thinks about that. 'Thirty-five million?'

'Thirty-six.'

'That's twelve million for each ticket.'

They stare at one another, not speaking. Anything is possible is what they don't say.

All the way to New York the snow goes on falling, the ploughs along the highways and on the turnpike working to clear it and scatter salt. For a time it freezes as it falls and the driver can't go faster than twenty. The vehicles keep a respectful distance from one another. Now and then a car up ahead goes into a graceful slow-motion skid, sliding and circling away out of the traffic into trees or bank or ditches.

Then, quite suddenly, the surface seems to thaw. The snow falls and melts. They pick up speed. 'We'll make it,' the driver says, as Henry takes his last look across the water at Manhattan's alphabet on a pale page of sky.

When they reach the terminal Henry pushes twenty dollars into the driver's hand. The driver thanks him. 'And I'm to give you this, Professor Bulov.'

It is a sheet of paper with a typewritten message, in capitals and with no signature:

HENRY: ASHTREE IS DEAD, AND STAYS [REPEAT: STAYS] DEAD. HE KEEPS HIS FAME AND YOU KEEP THE FLAME – BEST FOR US BOTH, NO? REPUTATION IS AN INVENTION. WE, YOU AND I, HAVE THE PATENT ON THIS ONE. LET'S KEEP IT THAT WAY.

ME, I GO AWAY, A LONG WAY, FOR A LITTLE R & R AND A LOT OF QUIET COMFORT.

And then, in lower case, are the lines from Keats Albie has quoted or referred to more than once:

> *Bold Lover, never never canst thou kiss*
> *Though winning near the goal, yet do not grieve,*
> *She cannot fade, though thou has not thy bliss.*
> *For ever wilt thou love, and she be fair!*

Who is the 'she'? Henry asks himself. He would like to think it refers to Joy, but he knows it doesn't. The 'she' for Albie is, must always have been, Fame.

The driver is already at the door of the limo, opening it to get in. 'When did he give you this?' Henry asks.

'I'm sorry, Sir. I'm not supposed to say.'

'It was Albie. Albie Strong.'

The driver stares at him, embarrassed at not being free to reply.

'You drove him up here in the night.'

'I'm sorry,' he says, and slides down into his seat.

Henry walks around the car and knocks on the window. The driver lowers it. 'I'm sorry, Sir,' he says again, shaking his head in refusal.

'Just tell me this,' Henry says. 'I'm not asking who, or when. But the person who gave you this message for me – did he give you an unusually large tip?'

Silence.

Henry is holding another twenty-dollar bill close to his nose. 'Very large, wasn't it?'

The driver looks away, embarrassed. 'I'm sorry. Please excuse . . .' He presses a button and the window slides up between them. He puts the car into drive and slides gently away from Henry, forward, and then out into the traffic.

Henry – Professor Bulov – international expert on the poetry of Alban Ashtree, a scholar of modest means who always travels economy, or as American Airlines call it, coach, is not surprised on this occasion to be told at the check-in that he has been upgraded.

'To business?'

'To first,' the attendant says, smiling.

'Ah,' he says. 'My fairy godmother.' And he guesses it will be the same all the way back to New Zealand.